Other titles from Riverfeet Press

THIS SIDE OF A WILDERNESS: A Novel (2013), by Daniel J. Rice

THE UNPEOPLED SEASON: *Journal from a North Country Wilderness* (2014), by Daniel J. Rice

WITHIN THESE WOODS (2015), by Timothy Goodwin
A collection of Northwoods nature essays, with original illustrations by the author.

THE UNPEOPLED SEASON: Collector's Edition (2015) by Daniel J. Rice
Includes 11 full-color images from the adventure.

available wherever books are sold, or on our webpage:
www.riverfeetpress.com

RELENTLESS

A Striker Mystery Novel

by Marcus Bruning

&

Jen Wright

Riverfeet Press
918 4th St SE
Bemidji, MN 56601
www.riverfeetpress.com

RELENTLESS
Marcus Bruning & Jen Wright
Copyright 2015 © by the authors
Edited by Daniel J. Rice and Charlene Brown
All rights reserved.

ISBN-13: 978-0-9963094-0-0
ISBN-10: 0996309403
LCCN: 2015958409

Riverfeet Press logo illustration by Timothy Goodwin
Cover design by Daniel J. Rice
Cover photograph by Dennis O'Hara
www.northernimages.com

Marcus Bruning dedicates this book to Jen Wright.

Jen's passion for life and dedication to helping those in need is indeed awe-inspiring.

Fishing the Favored Pond

Chapter 1

Strange as it may seem, I was enjoying myself on traffic patrol that day. Unlike other cops who might consider the assignment boring or demeaning, I loved it. To me, enforcing safe driving on the highways felt almost like recreation.

Like fishing. My lake of choice was a straight stretch of smooth interstate, rural with plenty of cover. My boat was a police-package stealth machine wrapped in maroon with a custom motor, transmission, and a purpose-designed drive-shaft. My ride had cop brakes and rotors and speed-rated Pirelli tires. With steering and suspension finely tuned for acceleration, this cruiser had nothing to do with comfort. I felt every bump as I crossed the expansion joints of the concrete. My fish-finder was a Stalker dual-head radar unit with forward and rear speed-measuring cones paired with a Vascar time and distance calculator. I sat poised to catch, but I didn't entice the fish to bite. I watched.

My focus was relaxed compared to the daily grind. I had volunteered for this HEAT shift (High-intensity Enforcement and Traffic) on overtime as extra duty. I almost felt guilty for collecting the time and a half. More sport than my usual duties as a detective in the major crimes unit, minding this speed trap felt more like play than work. For the past three years, theft, swindling, and property offenses had occupied my every thought and action. I rarely went home with the closure, there was always more to do. The sense of closure on a case was always overshadowed by the knowledge that a pile of unsolved cases sat on my desk, waiting. I often miss the early days of my career—those first twelve years of traffic enforcement and regular beat patrolling. I had closure every day. There was more to do, but it could wait. Much like fishing.

On traffic patrol that early summer day in Duluth, Minnesota, I didn't mind that I was fishing alone. I relaxed into the familiar and comfortable seat of my cruiser, enjoying the sixty-five degree weather. Inhabitants of this northern city would be ecstatic after the long winter spent sheltered indoors. Exuberant to leave the ice-cold, negative thirty degree temps and minus fifty wind chills, they were likely to express their joy in the speed at which they descended the hill into Duluth from I-35 South. Freshly rain-washed roads were free of winter's salt and sand, and the sky was cloudless as I watched, grateful not to be behind a desk. Nothing cleared my head like traffic patrol. If I had a partner riding along, we'd talk about sports, the weather, our relationships, other people's relationships, and tell stories—some of them true and some of them bullshit. It's part of fishing.

Fishing alone allowed me to think and to review my latest

cases. I'd just finished a lengthy identity theft/elder abuse investigation and was pleased with how the case had buttoned up. We had videotaped evidence of the perp cashing checks, and a tidy paper trail of online banking showing how he had bilked his wife's mother of her life savings while she was in rehab after a stroke. He'd moved or spent over two hundred thousand dollars in a three week period. Mr. Leech, as I liked to refer to him, was tucked into a cell at the jail and had already given a partial confession. My plan was to finish my reports on the case during this OT shift. In the relatively slow first few hours, I wrapped it up.

My squad was parked just over the Thompson Hill rise so that drivers would find themselves on top of me before they realized it, with no time to slow down. I could also get a good view of the harbor and ships entering the Twin Ports of Duluth-Superior over my shoulder or slip into the woods if I needed to take a leak. The port activity had been busy on this early summer day, and the lift bridge had moved up and down several times to let in a thousand-foot ore vessel and several smaller fishing and sailing boats. The high bridge was also visible from this vantage point. With such a spectacular view, the Thompson Hill rest area had become a popular make-out spot for the young and the cheating. But they weren't my focus.

The fishing seemed pretty average. Traffic was light. My twenty-two years of experience allowed me to guestimate the speed of oncoming cars to within a mile or two per hour. After making a guess, I would activate my radar, which sent back an audible tone and displayed the target's speed. The higher the tone, the higher the speed.

I played catch and release throughout the morning, as most of the drivers were traveling within an acceptable speed range. I'd stop and warn them and issue a no-seat-belt ticket to those who didn't even have enough sense to buckle up once stopped. Everyone speeds except for the occasional grandma or grandpa or the ultraliberal hybrid yuppie. My rule is, "Eight you're great; nine you're mine."I caught a few at nine or more over the posted seventy miles per-hour limit.

I liked to believe I was making a difference in keeping the would-be speeders safe as well as unwitting victims of drunk and distracted drivers. At an annual conference for law enforcement, prosecutors, judges, and probation officers, we were presented with sobering information about fatal crashes and the number of lives saved by traffic enforcement. That served as a critical motivator.

With an hour to go in my HEAT shift, I was sitting in the median about eight miles south of Duluth monitoring the northbound traffic when a lone headlight sliced through the mid-morning light. This bike was flying. *"Holy shit!"*I didn't even have time for a guess, activating the front cone when the radar screamed a high-pitched tone just below dog-audible-only. One hundred and forty miles per hour! The single occupant of a yellow, foreign crotch rocket looked right at me as he passed. The plate was a blur. I pointed my ship north, slammed my foot to the floor, and unleashed the power under my hood. A quarter mile later, I hit ninety and climbing. My siren, strobe lights, and LEDs, along with the sound of the engine, detonated the quiet countryside.

The rider had a decision to make. I was intent on catching him. *Would he stop, or would he run?*

I radioed dispatch and informed area cars about the catch I had on my line. Other units were a few miles north of me and converging. He wasn't slowing, and I passed a northbound car in the right lane like it was stopped. My instruments read one hundred forty-six miles per hour; good oil pressure and temperature. My machine was doing what it was made to do. I was doing what I had been trained to do and had done hundreds of times before, but what about him? He likely never, or perhaps only a couple of times in his life, had operated a vehicle that fast. His machine had probably not been maintained and constantly checked for optimal performance like mine.

Don't crash…. Don't crash, kid. Department policy required me to constantly balance the benefit of capture versus the risk to society. They called it "the balance test."*If I stop pursuing, will he stop running? Chances are he will.* Researchers tell us that it's like when a dog chases you. Most humans run. *On the other hand, why wouldn't he just stop? Why is he running? Is there another issue? Did he commit a crime, and he's trying to get away? Is the vehicle stolen? Is he armed or carrying drugs?* My machine was almost at its absolute limit. Traffic was light, but we veered toward a populated area. If he continued much more, I'd terminate the pursuit, but I needed to get close enough to read the plate.

The rider took an exit. I was a quarter mile behind him, and another squad driven by my partner Walt was southbound two miles ahead. Taking the exit, I scrubbed off speed rapidly, moving down the ramp. When I reached the cross, I looked left and right, but he was gone. My gut told me he likely reentered the northbound freeway. I punched the accelerator and headed back up the ramp at top speed. As I merged onto the freeway, I saw nothing but Walt moving toward me in the opposite lane. Over the radio I heard our local game warden Mickey calling in from a mile behind me: "Striker, he's southbound!" Mickey often backed us up when anything exciting came across the scanner. The guy's life could get a little dull.

I needed to turn around, so I grabbed some grass with my cruiser and headed south. This was no longer a leisurely fishing expedition. Walt and I rocketed into formation like two Blue Angels gaining on Mickey and the biker. Mickey announced that our target had taken the exit at 219. Another local officer reported in, approaching the intersection from the west. When we came down the ramp hot, the rider was nowhere in sight. Mickey radioed he'd seen nothing. Walt backed up the ramp and spotted tracks in the grass.

I jumped out and ran to where Walt was pointing. The Rocket was lying in the tall grass with no sign of impact. My neck hairs stood up. The kid could be anywhere: armed. I drew my gun and searched the tree line with my eyes and ears. The freeway noise made it impossible to hear movement in the grass or woods. I felt that sensation known only to cops and military personnel engaged in combat. *There's a very good possibility he's looking at me right now, and I can't see him. If he wanted to snipe me, I'm a sitting duck.*

Mickey joined us and spotted something in the brush. Walt shouted at the suspect to come out. A young voice responded, "Okay, okay," and he walked out on shaky legs with his hands over his head. We called off the rest of the cavalry.

After I cuffed him, I removed his helmet, freeing a mop of curly, light sandy brown hair and discovering what I had pretty much expected: a scared sixteen year old on the verge of bawling. I stuffed the boy in the back of my ticking cruiser. Mickey, Walt, and I stood on the shoulder reliving the chase. In the law enforcement world, we call this "cussing and discussing."

Walt waited on the tow truck, and I headed to the jail. Once there, I searched the rider again and uncuffed him, sitting him in an interview room where I booked him in myself. He was five foot ten and one hundred and fifty pounds of post-pubescent energy, but his eyes were wide with fear.

"So, why did you run?"

"I wanted to quit, but I didn't know how. I was afraid I was going to get killed."

"You endangered many more lives than your own today, including mine. When you first saw me, you should have stopped. You could have gotten off with a reckless driving ticket, and you would've been on your way. Instead, you ran. Now you're facing a felony, a weekend in jail, and your motorcycle's been forfeited. You made a horrible choice," I said in my cop voice. I stopped short of hard-ass mode because it was pretty clear he was a decent kid who'd screwed up—a good kid who'd made a bad decision. In my job, I come into contact with a lot of people making bad or impulsive decisions. For killers and rapists, and all breeds of sociopaths, the problem isn't about bad choices. It's about being pathologically deviant and having no empathy and no sense of right or wrong. Those people are actually few and far between. If there were more of them, I couldn't be a cop.

I lodged the kid at the jail and completed the pursuit and forfeiture reports. I drove the short distance from the jail to the brand-spanking-new law enforcement center and turned in my cruiser, spending a few minutes putting the finishing touches on my elder abuse case. On my way out, I threw the file on my lieutenant's desk. "Signed, sealed, and delivered."

"I'm sure it's excellent." Lieutenant Gerard said. "That's why I'm moving you." My heart jumped in my chest. "Moving me?" *Where the hell would he move me to?*

"We're reorganizing: starting a violent crimes unit." He looked at me for a response. I tilted my head like one of our police canines did when he was trying to understand my words.

"As in domestics specifically?" I finally croaked out.

With a long history of training on the dynamics of domestic violence(DV), I knew that most cases of assault involved a victim and an assailant known to each other, usually from the same family. The training I did as a side consulting job allowed me to travel and to get away from the daily grind. I trained cops in multiple states as part of a Department of Justice program over the last ten years. Because of it, I felt like I spent a great deal of my life thinking about violence. I didn't want my entire work life focused on it too.

"That's exactly what I'm talking about. We've seen an upswing in DV calls and arrests since you trained our street officers. John Q. Public isn't going to get that. He'll just see more domestics and blame us. We've also got to get a handle on the stalking laws out there. The chief's wife is on the board of the women's shelter, and I'm feeling some pressure to answer to him. You're the man for the job, Kevin Arthur Dexter. This is your thing. You can make us shine."

I must have looked a little shocked because he scrunched his eyebrows at me. He knew my whole name, which was a sure sign he'd been digging in my file. Even more shocking was the part about being moved. Cops hate two things: One-the way things are and two-change.

"You do like the idea, don't you?"

"All due respect here, sir, it's just a little sudden. I need some time to adjust to the idea. I've kind of always liked the variety in the major crimes unit and having a break from the DV stuff. This will mean eating and breathing it."

"I'm sorry, Dexter, it's a done deal. Monday you head the new unit."

"Head as in a promotion or head as in a new title?"

"Title… and a car to drive home." He smiled weakly. "A new car."

"How many in the unit?"

"You and Smith."

"Monday?"

He nodded.

I knew a little about Smith but not much. He was known as a computer geek with a lot of Military and combat experience. Rumor had it that he had a lot of baggage from the combat. I mentally committed to being open minded. The computer stuff would definitely be a plus.

Breaking the News

Chapter 2

I took the long way to my Chester Park home, thinking about this new duty, pondering my career and the direction it had taken.

I chose to go into law enforcement after attending an Explorers Expo sponsored by my high school. Explorers is a Boy Scout program designed to give young adults ages fifteen to twenty-one an opportunity to try out various careers to see which they might like to pursue. I got to ride along with several police officers, and the excitement and variety of the job appealed to me. I found that I had a knack for dealing with the unexpected people and situations encountered every day in law enforcement. It was a different path from the ones most of my friends took, but it gave me a sense of strength and purpose as I struggled to find my way. Back then, I was a boy prone to rowdy behavior. Although the officers I rode along with have all since retired, they were the role models who led me to a career I have enjoyed all of my adult life.

People I don't know very well often look at me in an odd way when they learn I'm a cop, sometimes suspiciously, as though I have something to hide or might know their own dark secrets. The fact is, I like my job, and I'm a pretty normal person. The job is filled with highs. We help people out when they don't know what else to do or where to turn when things go bad. They call us when they've been wronged or hurt—when they've exhausted their abilities to resolve an issue or a conflict. They call us when things aren't going well—when they need a referee or a decision maker. We resolve conflicts and set the score straight. We intervene to impose a consequence or interpret a rule, whether of law or custom. Sometimes we act as parent and occasionally savior.

Most of the citizens I've dealt with are decent people who've made a bad choice. It's best if I treat them that way. Thinking that people are generally bad leads to burnout, and I've seen many cops fall victim to anger and frustration, their disrespect taking them down along with the stress.

The job can also be about being there for the good times. I've assisted newborn babies to arrive safely into the world. I've saved a few lives, but that's the exception, not the rule. The department has given me two Life-Saver awards, and they sit on my home office shelf, mostly forgotten. I'm not a superhero. I'm a typical cop. It's what we do.

Everyone (except cops and former cops) has a fairly skewed picture in mind about police work and about what we are like. Unfortunately, that opinion has been formed by watching movies or television shows that depict cops involved in highly dramatic episodes. People don't associate police work with calm, intelligent problem solvers. More likely, they think of shows like *Cops* or *America's Most Wanted*, in which officers fight and wrestle their way through a shift. Most of the time, law enforcement is a thinking and communication profession requiring very little brawn. People are generally respectful toward the police while being somewhat suspicious of our intentions. Still, antisocial elements feel the need to fight and resist.

As a kid, I was involved in an occasional fight throughout my school-aged days in the eastern neighborhoods of Duluth, but I was never really trained to be a fighter. The police academy physically prepared me to do battle. I learned how to protect myself and to control people no matter how resistive they might become. The training allowed me to start the job knowing how to defend myself, but my skills at reading aggression in people had to be developed. I learned early on that some people wanted to hurt me.

My fellow officers won some and occasionally lost some of the physical altercations with disorderly citizens of our fair city. I developed a mindset and eventually the skills to always win. Well, almost always. Most of the time I could talk my way into deescalating a situation, but I quickly learned when it was "go time." I developed what I refer to as my golden rules: *Don't fight fair, fight to win. Strike first when necessary, and always do what you need to do to arrive safely home at the end of a shift.*

The rules served me well, but the striking first thing caused me some grief. I had learned how to read aggression, and fighting fair didn't apply. I didn't need to get hit before I could strike. More than one Internal Affairs investigation was launched over complaints against me, but I always came out clean. I didn't violate anyone's rights or behave unethically. I was just one step ahead of the aggression. That's how I got my nickname "Striker." Oddly enough, the first person to call me by that name was an Internal Affairs investigator. I had been put on administrative leave following an incident in which a six-foot six-inch, roughly four hundred pound crook resisted arrest and ended up with a dislocated shoulder and a broken nose. I'm no Tiny Tim myself at six-foot four, but I came away without a scratch. There were no video cameras in the area, so it was essentially my word against his.

We received a call about a car prowler breaking into cars in a remote parking area on a segment of the Lake Superior Hiking Trail. The parking area abutted the property of an observant neighbor who heard the sound of breaking glass. I was close by. I made the assumption that it was a kid and went in quickly. I parked my squad a short distance from the lot and hiked in. I came right up on the burglar with a crowbar in his grip about to slam it into the driver's side window of a Honda CRV with liberal stickers plastering the bumper. I identified myself as a police officer. Rather than lowering the crowbar, he tightened his grip. I started another verbal command, hoping he would believe I was going to give him one more chance. Instead, I gave him a quick punch to the face followed by a straight-arm hold, bringing him face down. I felt his shoulder go as I pushed him to the ground.

His version of the story was that I went ballistic without giving him a chance to drop the bar. He claimed that because he was big, I responded with overkill, doing more damage than was necessary. Anyway, the long and short of it, according to the Internal Affairs guy, was that my attitude about not giving a goon with a crowbar the chance to ring my bell before I acted earned me a reputation, and a new nickname. He dubbed me Striker, and it stuck.

The weird part of my job, and maybe what makes people wonder, is the horror I've experienced. I truly believe that human beings are supposed to experience very few horrific events in their lifetime. My number greatly exceeds that. When bad things happen and people run away, I move toward the trouble. I've seen death, both gruesome and peaceful. Suicides are not uncommon, along with the family members who will never understand. The hours spent in the room with a person who died peacefully while I waited for a family member to arrive are permanently etched into my memory. My experience with death has made me think seriously about the meaning of life. What questions will we be asked when we meet our maker? Did we love well? Freely? What impacts and influences have we had and upon whom? To me, the body is a vehicle. Remembering this helps to keep my head on straight. I rarely become emotionally involved when I can maintain that perspective.

The really nasty scenes have left indelible marks, though. I don't know if anyone else can see them, but I know they're there. Don't believe someone who tells you that human carnage doesn't bother them.

One such mark was left by the first bad crash I witnessed. A young woman had rolled her car because she was paying attention to her phone rather than the road. The top caved in and the steering wheel pinned her. She suffered excruciating pain before dying in front of me while we waited for paramedics and fire to arrive. It was horrible. I made it through the event, but I relive the experience to some degree every time I pass that location. The problem is, the number of those tragic events has grown over the years. I call them intrusional memories. They pop up at the strangest times, and I zone out. Maybe that's why I've noticed people looking at me as though I have secrets. Maybe I do, but I've been trained to be stoic and to hide any emotion. I only wish I could turn that skill off when I'm not on the job. It's hard. It makes me different. And sometimes it makes me feel alone.

When I got home, my girlfriend Georgia stood in the kitchen and asked me to join her, but I mumbled something and went into the bedroom. I needed a few minutes to decide how I was going to share the news with her. Changing into shorts and a T-shirt, I grabbed a beer from the fridge and turned on the TV. Georgia stood behind me without saying a word. She was accustomed to my silence.

The news coverage was all about local crime. I pondered why our culture needed to know about and even glorify every serious crime that happened in our city. My job as a detective put me smack dab in the middle of it all. I jabbed the remote, turning the station. Every other channel hyped true crime, or the kind of fictional crime that gives the public unrealistic expectations of evidence collection and prosecution standards. I tuned the TV to a music station, got up, selected whole-house surround sound, and was drawn into the kitchen by the smell of garlic.

Georgia was cooking up some kind of an Italian pasta dish that made my mouth water. Since she'd moved in a year before, I'd had to work very hard to limit my weight gain. Her love for cooking and baking kept me working out like a fiend. We'd dated for a year before she moved in, and the benefits of home cooking were definitely worth the extra poundage and workouts.

"Nice," she said to my music choice.

"Nice," I said as I looked into her eyes and touched her cheek. Every night I questioned her commitment to me. Not because she had said or done anything to make me question it. Every guy who worked in major crimes was either divorced or on the brink because of the long and unpredictable hours. So far, we'd been able to dial into a rhythm of connecting or taking off on a road trip in between major investigations, but I wasn't holding my breath.

She was tall at five-foot eight—smoking hot, smart, and a passionate lover. I towered over her, but her unique combination of toned lean muscle and gentle curves made my knees weak. Her dark hair and sea-green eyes could look right through me.

Even though I did everything in my power to make sure she knew she was a priority, I kept waiting to see the first crack in the armor. She could have her pick of guys, and couldn't figure out what she saw in a hulk like me. My big frame and beefy paws helped get me out of many a potential scrape as a cop, but I wasn't a stud by any stretch of the imagination. I had started to sport a gut in the last year due to her cooking, despite my taking trips to the gym every other day, and my three-mile runs several times a week.

I worried about this new assignment. *Would the hours be worse? Would I be able to keep some sense of mental health while surrounded by seriously violent relationships?* Georgia's occupation as a therapist also made me question my ability to stay connected to her. She'd been more emotionally present than anyone I had ever been involved with before, but given my profession, I hadn't been able to share myself so openly. My tendency was to shut down or tune out and focus on something else when anything was bothering me. The few times I had talked about and worked through tough situations with her, she'd been there for me. If I could open up like that more often, it would probably be good for us, but I always felt like I fell short in that department.

I decided to start our chat with the second thing on my mind. "I got in a pursuit today with a dipshit on a motorcycle who reminded me of Alex."

"Alex your son or Alex from the feds?"

"Mini-me. This kid was a little older but seemed to be running on pure instinct, trying to find his way. He bought a sport bike three weeks ago and, like every other kid, had to see how fast it would go."

"Don't tell me he ended up dying, "she said, as she moved about the kitchen opening windows to let in some of the fresh, clean air.

"Nobody got hurt, but he made a judgment error that will likely haunt him the rest of his life. He's going to have a felony on his Juvenile record, unless they defer it, which they probably will."

"He loses the bike, too, doesn't he?"

"Yeah. He put four grand down on it. That was a shitty investment."

"Yeah, but he could be dead. Did you wrap up that case with the creep stealing from his mother-in-law?"

"Uh-huh. The guy rolled like a weasel on himself, hoping his wife would take pity. The good news is he's in jail, but the bad news is his mother-in-law's savings is gone forever. I got to think Christmas is going to suck for both of them." I snatched a piece of the freshly cut garlic bread.

"Nice. Very nice."

"The lieutenant called me in today," I said, sniffing around the kitchen like a predator looking for a chance to sample what smelled so good, circling the conversation in my mind.

"Oh yeah?"

"He likes my work—says he wants me to head a new unit."

"He's making you chief?" she said, swatting my hand away from grabbing another piece of bread.

I pulled a saddle stool up to the island. "No. He told me he's getting pressure from the boss—whose wife is on the board of the women's shelter—to start a violent crimes unit. The main focus will be on domestic violence and stalking. It'll be me and Smith, and I'm running it."

"Is it a promotion?"

"That's what I asked. It's basically a new hat. Oh, and a take-home."

"Great. Now we get to have a cruiser sitting in the yard? The neighbors already look at us like we're from Mars."

"Nah, it'll be something a little less obvious than that. Honestly, I don't mind some of the neighbors being a little nervous. It's better than when I was their personal cop, with them coming to me tattling their little grievances about each other. They acted like I was part priest, part talk show host, telling me about someone they knew speeding through residential areas or some other stupid shit. Now they're afraid I'm above all that. I'm an investigator, and maybe I'll turn them in for something serious."

"You're a goofball. I actually think we're lucky to have most of the neighbors we do. Buck and Jenny are some of our best friends, and the monthly neighborhood theme parties are sweet." She laughed as she pulled an amazing garlic-laden dish of lasagna from the oven.

"What are you laughing at?"

"Remember the theme party last fall—the one where the guests had to come dressed in a costume that began with the letter P? You were the Pope, and I was a smokin' hot prostitute. Quite a combo."

"You're always smokin' hot. You didn't even have to dress up," I said, running my hand up her tight behind. She smacked me with the spatula she had at the ready to cut into the Italian delicacy.

"No tastes," she said as I wrapped my arms around her and pulled her close.

"Maybe not the full meal deal, but how about an hors d'oeuvre?"

She moved the now messy spatula between my face and hers.

"Maybe later?" I released her and watched her fine form walk toward the table.

"Maybe," she said, looking back over her shoulder, totally busting my gawk. I poured us each some wine and sat facing her. The food was fantastic as usual.

"Why Smith?"

"What?" I was lost in the food like a black bear in the fall discovering a thick patch of blueberries.

"Why did the lieutenant partner you with Smith?"

"Oh, yeah, I guess we make the glory team. The chief knows I'm doing all that training on DV and shining the spotlight on our agency, and Smitty's just back from the sand. I think that was his third deployment. At least he's single. I can't imagine leaving a family behind to go fight some war over oil."

"Single and a widower are two very different things. Maybe he keeps volunteering for war to avoid his personal battles." Her perspective as a therapist definitely held some weight here. I'd learned early on that she was usually right about people and their motives.

"It sucks that his wife died. Maybe the battle zone keeps his mind occupied. He doesn't seem to mind the fuss over his war decorations, either. He's kind of an adrenaline junky and maybe a little off."

"You all are."

"Thanks a lot! Anyway, I think we'll make a pretty decent team. I'll help him with the dynamics of battering and get him over his victim blaming mentality, and he can get me up to speed on the technology. Gerard specifically mentioned the stalking thing, and so much of that is related to electronics—cell phones, the Internet, GPS, cameras, and tracking crap. It's scary what people can do these days."

"How're you feeling about it?" she asked, loading my plate with another helping.

"I don't like being volun-told, but I won't mind bringing some accountability down on these guys. I'm just not sure I want to be doing DV full-time. I'll miss the crooks. And I'm not sure I want to be immersed in DV at work as well as when I'm training." I was talking about work, but my mind had turned its attention back to lust. That must have shone through in the way I was looking at her.

"It's not later yet, hon.," she said, touching my arm. "Maybe after you've done the dishes. I'm going downstairs to practice my karate."

I rushed through the dishes and crept down the stairs to watch her. She went through a series of slow-motion moves before jumping up into a two-legged kick. I found her strength and determination totally hot.

Shortly after she moved in, Georgia helped me remodel the basement. We turned the cinderblock lower level into a spacious television/workout room. It was carpeted, sheet-rocked, and had a cedar ceiling and diagonal accent wall. It was roomy enough for her to practice her karate, and I had a treadmill and some weights set up. The weights weren't much, but they were enough to keep my joints moving in-between getting to the full gym at the police station.

"Do you want to help?" she asked.

I bounced up. "Sure."

"Try to hit me. Start over there," she pointed toward the stairs, "and come at me fast."

I was a little hesitant, given my size and training, so I think I was a tad tentative, but I took three large steps and threw a balled-hand punch at her. She used my forward motion, applied straight-arm pressure, and pinned me down to the carpet.

"Sorry, hon.," she said, as I got up, gingerly rubbing my shoulder. "But could you come at me a little harder? You know, like you mean it."

The only thing I really meant was to get her into bed and show her some moves of my own, but I said, "I'll try, but I'm going to have to think of some creep. You know what this stuff does to me." I pulled her close and felt the heat build between us.

I remembered when I first laid eyes on her at one of my softball tournaments several years before. I had pegged her as a snob—someone shallow, good-looking, and totally un-reachable. She joined our group at the sponsor's bar after the game, and we struck up a conversation. I was surprised at how physically attracted to her I was during that first conversation. I felt my body involuntarily leaning into her, and I nearly kissed her. She asked me about my work, and I found her to be an easy conversationalist and a good listener. As the evening went on, I had this overpowering feeling that all was right with the world. It was easy. I found myself telling her things I had never told anyone. Things I had barely told myself.

The whole week following that game, I thought about her incessantly. I built up my courage, tracked down her number, and called, asking her for a date. We ended up going for a walk on the Lakewalk and then out to dinner at a local Thai place. The deep talks continued. She didn't treat me like a therapy client, or I would have ran.

Cops don't like shrinks. A poor psychological evaluation is the quickest way to lose your career, or your reputation. I had never talked to a head doc, but I had struggles, and Georgia had a way of probing within my comfort zone. I had been in a few relationships over the years but had never let anyone get too close. That probably had something to do with my work life but also stemmed from the sting I was dealt while still a senior in high school.

I was partying pretty hard and living life for the moment

like most high school kids do. The game changer for me was when the girl I was seeing, Annette, told me she thought she was pregnant. I remember telling her to chill out and take a pregnancy test—sure that it would reveal she was wrong. The test indicated positive, and my life changed forever. I started thinking about the future and was terrified at the prospect of having to be a grown-up.

Unfortunately, Annette didn't grasp the same concept or face her fears in a productive way. She continued to party throughout the pregnancy and pushed me away when I confronted her. We had some nasty arguments, and our relationship was pretty much over by the time our son Alex came along. He was born deaf, and Annette slipped further into the partying world, probably as an escape. She got arrested about six months after Alex was born, on drug trafficking and possession. Annette went to prison, served forty-eight months, and came out to reengage the drug lifestyle. She completely abandoned us and seemed even to deny our existence. I was left with Alex and a real fear of letting anyone get too close.

Now Alex is eighteen going on twelve, and living on his own in the Duluth Hillside neighborhood in low rent housing with some friends. His emotional struggles, impulsive behavior, and aggression are fueled in part by his physical disability. No doubt he has a sense of abandonment, too. Some of his issues are due to circumstance, but although no pathologist will confirm it, I firmly believe the drug use during pregnancy was a serious contributing factor. Annette is out of our lives and will be forever. I wrestle with a deep resentment but channel that energy into working with Alex. Our relationship is tenuous at best. He is hot and cold toward me and the world, prone to anger barely under his control.

When we met, Georgia asked me all the right questions and was careful not to push too hard. She listened, but more important, she challenged me. The rest is history. She made me want to be a better person.

As we made physical contact, I moved back into the present. I was more than a little weak in the knees and knew that I would be of no further help to her as she practiced her karate techniques. "I'm sorry, babe, but I'm not going to be much help here."

"I know precisely what this does to you," she said with a thick voice as she led me upstairs.

"That's not why I practice with you, but it is a nice fringe benefit."

"Your benefit package isn't so bad yourself."

Once we finished our lovemaking and untangled from the sheets, she told me about a difficult case she was dealing with in her therapy practice. A woman had come to her because she was having difficulty sleeping. The client said that she had pretty much written it off to postmenopausal hormonal dips. Georgia suspected, however, that a lack of sleep wasn't enough to motivate a first-time foray into therapy.

When the client did sleep, her dreams could turn bizarre. She often awoke gasping for breath after dreaming about drowning in the water or falling from a cliff. Georgia encouraged her to undergo a sleep study to determine if sleep apnea had been the cause of her gasping for breath, but no sleep abnormalities were found. The woman was in a long-term monogamous relationship with a man she truly liked, and her work was relatively satisfying. The woman became agitated and slightly defensive when probed about her childhood, so Georgia was slowly exploring that avenue.

She told me that the most difficult part about her work was being able to correctly gage if someone was ready and emotionally strong enough to turn over a rock that had been hiding a problem for decades. On the one hand, the client wasn't sleeping, so the issue was presented. This usually meant that the person was ready and able to explore the issue. The person's previous experience and level of coping skills also played a part in how and when he or she would be able to uncover buried trauma. The scariest part for the therapist was helping the patient through the stress of it all. This woman had begun stealing. Georgia described her as a solid, relatively well-respected public figure who had begun shoplifting and taking small items from those close to her. Georgia hoped that she could help her client to navigate this without losing everything she had built in her life to this point.

I had learned that my role when Georgia talked about her clients was to listen, to hold her emotional pain, and to let her vent. I learned that lesson the hard way. Early on, I had tried to solve every problem she brought to me. That's what cops do. People bring you problems; you solve them. My solutions were met with less than positive results.

I gently stroked her hair as she wound down her tale of the woman's situation. She snuggled closer into my arms, and I kissed her forehead.

"You are so patient and kind," I said.

"And you are a good listener," she said, and we both drifted off to sleep.

She's Gone

Chapter 3

Smitty was at the desk facing mine first thing on Monday morning. While the new cop shop was gorgeous, and the chief had a large office overlooking a pond, the lowly detectives were all situated in cubicles in a bullpen. The arrangement was intentional. We were not encouraged to get so comfortable that we would hang around the office doing "paperwork" too often. The desks were arranged two by two so that partners could easily converse yet have private desks. The building was more spacious than the old station in downtown Duluth's City Hall. The old location had a view of the lift bridge and the hillside to the north, but it was over a hundred years old and in need of a gut job.

"Hey, Striker, glad to be working with you," Smitty said with a handshake. "Got us some of the good stuff." He pointed to the Starbucks on my desk. "Figured you deserved a cup of coffee for having to put up with me."

"You definitely have a point," I said with a smile. "I'm not sure one cup will actually be enough compensation, do you?" I took a swig of the dark roast. *Starbucks and a day-old dough-nut. The breakfast of champions.*

"You're right. I should probably invest in a franchise. We'll be drinking so much coffee that the job'll get done in half the time." He took his own big swig.

"Fuckers don't stand a chance," I said as I sat down and kicked back in my chair. "So here's what I'm thinking."

"Don't hurt yourself, boss. It's early."

"We can either clean up ongoing cases from the detectives or wait till new stuff comes in. If we take a couple of cases off the detectives, we get some points. If we take new ones, we could start clean. We want our clearance rate as high as we can get it. These are some tough cases, you know. Victims don't usually testify."

"Wow, clearance rate. I can see why they made you boss." He leaned back in his chair and put one foot up on his desk. "I say we start clean. The D's are getting enough of a break with us taking the new cases off their plate."

"What'd they give you for equipment?" I asked.

"Nothing so far. Just told me to pull my desk up."

"How about I go see the Lieu, get a car, and try to squeeze out a budget for electronics? That's your specialty, right?"

He sat up suddenly. "I'm the man. Give me a computer, phone, tracking device, wire, whatever. I'll make it better. We don't have it, give me a pile of parts, and I'll build it. Keep me in coffee, and I'll make sure even you know how to use it."

"I think you underestimate your task there, my friend," I said as I headed to the Lieu's desk. I liked Smitty's sense of humor, and I was smiling as I entered the lieutenant's formidable office. The old Central High School clock tower loomed behind him, and I could see a slice of Lake Superior out his large window. He wasn't in, but he had a note tacked to the end of his desk with my name on it. "Dexter, see Sandra for your car and keys to the supply room."

Sandra gave me a big smile as I approached—too big, in fact.

"What?"

"You have your first case, and it's a doozy." She raised her eyebrows sympathetically.

She handed me a set of car keys and a separate set for the electronics supply room. "You and Smith have to sign out everything you use. If you break it, you need to fill out an R9 report."

I nodded, anxiously awaiting details of the new case.

"Here's the address. It's Genevieve Sanders, and she's missing. She reported a possible stalker recently. Her father will get you up to speed. The lieutenant asked me to printout the matter of record and 911 calls from her during the past year." She handed me a crisp new file.

"The Genevieve Sanders from News 7?"

She nodded. "I watch that channel, so go find her alive. Please." She shooed me off.

It was a little unnerving to have a high-profile celebrity as the subject of my first case, and I wondered why the powers that be hadn't assigned this to missing persons. Maybe the stalking led the case assigner to direct it my way. I also wondered how long the upper brass had known about this new unit before I did. It would have been nice to be brought into the planning and to have roles spelled out more clearly before being thrown into our first investigation.

I picked up Smitty en route to our new car. We didn't even get a chance to revel in the beauty of the new loaded Impala before we headed to Mr. Sanders' home in the affluent neighborhood of Congdon. Situated on East Fourth Street, it was not so much a house as it was a three-story turn-of-the-century mansion.

As a native, I was well aware of all the class lines as they relate to the various neighborhoods in Duluth. Congdon property values and taxes were the highest of any neighborhood in the city. Large oak and maple trees bordered the ample yards. The Sanders mansion was a classic white clapboard-sided house with yellow trim. Its rounded entranceway was supported by two pristine white pillars. A small creek flowed behind the house, wending its way down the hill toward Lake Superior. I breathed in the calm serenity of the moment before we were buzzed through the gate by someone other than Mr. Sanders. As we neared the house, we were greeted by a formal butler.

"Right this way, gentlemen."

We silently followed him inside. The house smelled of polished wood and freshly brewed coffee. I enjoyed the homey feel that the smells elicited. It reminded me of the home Georgia and I shared.

Mr. Sanders was seated at a large dining room table overlooking the wooded back yard. He rose.

"Thanks for coming so quickly." He wrung his hands. He was tall and thin and somewhere in the sixty to seventy age range. His hair was mostly grey, and he wore tailored slacks and a stiffly pressed white shirt. His eyes were strained, and his temples throbbed like he had a migraine.

"You okay?" I had to ask.

"If you find Genevieve, I will be." He stroked his temple.

"Tell me everything you know. Start from the beginning," I prodded.

"She's had a stalker. I mean, a freak. Not your run-of-the-mill TV hero worshipper." He looked at us to see if we followed. I took out a small notebook to encourage him to supply details. "She's always had at least one nutcase trying to connect with her because she's a television reporter, you know. But this was different."

"How was this different?" I didn't want to lead him.

"This guy was more persistent, and she was afraid of him. She actually sat me down last week and told me all about it. She wanted me to know what was going on in case something happened to her." He stroked his temples again. "This guy was sending her flowers—to the station, to her home, and even to a restaurant where she dined regularly. She got up to use the bathroom, and a waiter placed a flower arrangement on her table. When she asked the waiter who had left it, he said that it had been delivered by a local florist with her name on it."

"I'll need the name of that restaurant, and of the florist, if you have it."

"I've written it all down for you." He handed me a manila envelope. "I hired a private detective when she came to me last week. A lot of good it did. The stalker took her. I'm sure of it. He left flowers for her everywhere, even here, and the private eye couldn't trace them. They were paid for with a disposable credit card purchased with cash, and the flowers were always purchased online. The PI tracked the email addresses, but they were new addresses created for one-time use. This guy knew what he was doing."

"Did he ever communicate with her in person other than sending the flowers?"

"No, that's the weird thing. She had no clue who it was."

"Any spurned boyfriends?"

"Plenty," he said. "I had the private eye check some of them out. It's all in there."

"Did he send any text messages? Emails?"

"He sent her clips of herself from the news. He edited them together so that they said, 'I want you. We are meant to be. This is important.' That's what really freaked her out. I think the copy is at her office. They did an analysis of the tape, and it's high end. Not just some video hack."

"How long has she been gone?"

"Two days."

"How did you come to believe she was missing?"

"She calls me every day. We're close. I haven't heard from her. She hasn't been to work. She never misses, and her car is still at her house. The sick bastard has her. There is no way that she wouldn't call me if something wasn't terribly wrong. I'm certain of it." He began to cry.

"Please just find her. Do whatever you have to. If you don't have the resources you need, see me. I'll pay for everything."

"No ransom demands?"

He straightened up. "Oh, my god, I didn't think of that. No, nothing. Would that fit with the flowers and the video?"

"Not really, but it pays to explore all angles." I wanted him to feel comforted by our thoroughness.

I thought of my son Alex. I could barely imagine the fear Sanders must have been going through. Alex had been attending a specialized boarding school for the deaf in southern Minnesota. Up until he turned eighteen, he used to come home most weekends. Now he had a girlfriend, was living on his own, and his visits were fewer and further apart. It had been hard on him when I started seeing Georgia—not because he didn't like her, but mostly because he didn't like change. He was hot tempered, and when I introduced her to him, he stormed out of the room. They had gained quite a bit of ground since then. Georgia was open and loving toward him, and well, everybody likes Georgia. She had learned enough sign so that she could communicate with him, and he was warming to her. Even though I didn't see him often, I still thought about him every day.

Detectives are cautioned not to make associations between victims and our own family members when investigating a case, as that can lead to impaired judgment and limited perspective, but I had yet to meet an investigator who could be that objective. The only ones who came close didn't have kids.

"Does she still have a room here?" Smitty asked.

"Sure does. Up the stairs, second door on the left. Help yourselves."

The room was a typical girl-grows-up room. She had high school yearbooks, scrapbooks, old letters and poetry, and barely used prom dresses in the closet. Smitty gathered up a few personal items for further review, and we left Sanders with a business card and instructions to call.

"One more thing," I asked Sanders. "What about her mother? Where can I find her?"

"She died when Genevieve was just a baby. My daughter is all I have now. Please find her."

On the way to the missing reporter's house, Smitty grilled me on stalker profiles. I explained that the perpetrator likely believed that Genevieve really wanted him or that his offerings would sway her to love him. He was likely someone she currently knew, had known, or had rejected. He would be controlling and might be operating in a fantasy world that he believed was reality, or that he could make reality by giving her gifts. He could be getting off on her fear, victimizing her for power if he felt scorned. His actions were meant to send a message like, "You can't escape me. I'm powerful."

I was worried that our missing reporter had been kidnapped. More than that, I was worried for her life. Stalking is at the top of the list of risk factors for femicide. Stalking and then kidnapping put her risk of being murdered sky high.

Her Woodland home was humble compared to her father's. She had a large lot that backed up to a creek, but other than that, it was a typical story-and-a-half bungalow. The neighborhood was middle class, made up of smaller housing stock built in the 1920's with a scattering of mid-century ranch homes. The area had its share of parks and quiet charm, but lacked the dramatic contours of the Duluth hillside neighborhood leading down to the big lake. In its favor, Woodland had one of the lowest crime rates in the city.

A Toyota Camry sat in the garage, and the house was spotless. It was too clean. There was nothing in any of the garbage cans, and every surface gleamed. The whole place smelled of disinfectant and bleach. I made a mental note to see if Ms. Sanders had a cleaning service. We could tell by the timing of the cleaning crew whether the crime scene had been erased. When we used luminal to search for blood, bleach would make the whole place light up. If someone had used bleach to erase the crime scene, I was going to have to dig deeper.

"Smitty. Let's get a search warrant. I want to pull the drains, and I highly doubt that Judge Lambert will see Daddy's consent to search as an okay to dig that deep." While I didn't suspect any family members, I knew from experience to be safe.

An hour later, we were back at the house, warrant in hand, along with the best technician from our criminal evidence and identification unit, known as ID for short, though the technicians are often called "paste-eaters" behind their backs. They gather evidence at the scene and meticulously analyze fiber, hair, blood, and other bodily fluids collected from victims and in the vicinity of a crime.

Kent Larsen was a ten-year cop who moved into law enforcement from the science world. I heard he was a chemistry teacher for a few years before coming to the DPD. I can't imagine he was a very good teacher, though, because his social skills were limited. Assigned to the ID unit for the last eight years or so, he had found his calling. He was the best man in the unit.

The ID officers are a different breed. Most are placed there because they don't fit in anywhere else in the department and don't have the people skills to be good cops. Most have Asperger's tendencies and are smart as a whip. However, for me and most investigator types, spending twelve hours in the same car with one of them would result in the high probability of at least one death, and a murder-suicide wasn't out of the question.

Fortunately, to be in ID you don't need social skills. You need to excel in weird science and attention to detail. These guys aren't misfits; they just fit in differently. I had come to appreciate their work but wasn't very good at telling them that. Larsen had never let me down, and I needed a break with this big case.

I called Genevieve's dad to let him know we were digging a little deeper and to ask him about the maid service. He said that Genevieve had a weekly housekeeper named Louise. I got the particulars.

Smitty and I worked together to cover all of the bases. Kent pulled the drains and collected hair and fibers. He left no stone unturned. We shot digital pictures of every room and created an inventory of what items we took with us for evidence. I told Smitty I wanted to take one more look to be sure I hadn't missed something. What I really wanted was to know Genevieve. I needed to get my head wrapped around who she was. I spent the next two hours sifting through every part of her private space. Smitty poked around in her garage.

I had always wondered about these news folks. Were they really the cool and calm face they portrayed, or were they merely puppets, pretending to show empathy and compassion while they read their carefully written scripts? I discovered Genevieve had a healthy case of vanity riddled with low self-esteem. She had hundreds of pictures of glam'd up celebrities and photos of herself in similar attire. It didn't matter if she was in a picture with friends on a night out or with family at the lake home, one thing was always constant: she looked well made up and was dressed perfectly.

I found yearbooks from high school and college. Each was completely filled with signatures and fond wishes. I found still photos and video from high school and campus news productions. She knew what she wanted, and she wanted to be seen. I found volumes of books covering every self-help topic known to humanity. How to be happy. How to be skinny. How to be popular. How to walk, sit, and stand. How to pick the perfect man. This one intrigued me. I wondered if I might learn what Georgia saw in me. After a minute of leafing through the book, I could see it was all about selecting someone to complement your look and to accentuate your strengths. I'll cross that book off Georgia's Christmas list.

I also saw a side of her that I didn't expect. She was into social change. She volunteered to help the needy. She had written some poetry that led me to believe there was a human being under the pretty wrapping.

Catching up with Smitty downstairs, I asked, "Anything good in the garage?"

"Nah. Some garage sale items. About what you would expect from a chick's garage. Especially a rich chick who has everything done for her. No tools or toys. Not even a rake or shovel. You find anything?"

"I did some digging to see who she really is. Best I can tell, she's a bit of a narcissist."

"You got that right."

"Yeah, but I found some stuff that surprised me. She clearly likes the attention but has a side I hadn't expected. She comes from money, right?"

"Yeah?"

"She could have traveled the world and been pampered with amenities. Instead, she took trips to third-world countries, helped to build schools and set up medical support. I don't think she was doing it for the fame. I had written her off as a high-maintenance brat, but now I'm thinking there's more to her. I found this poem she wrote. I'm not into poetry, but my impression of it was that she has been moving beyond the fame stuff. I seriously got a peek under the hood. Here is an example of some of her writing: *You are the sun on my face as I surface.* She was talking about her relationship with her father as she worked through an anxious time.

Smitty smirked at me. "A peek under the hood, huh? This chick is hot, and you're not the only one who would like to get a peek under her hood."

"Focus!" I shot him a glare. "We need to see her as a human being. Try to get into her head." I didn't think his turning her into a sex object would enhance his objectivity. I should have taken the opportunity to educate him about male privilege and how objectifying women was what the perpetrators did to justify their violence, but I needed to make some headway in this investigation fast.

"The poetry gave me a peek, but I was hoping for a diary or something. I went through her books pretty closely. I thought for sure she'd be the type who'd write volumes. It's like she just vanished. Her car's here, but her purse, keys, wallet, and cell phone are gone like she just went out for the evening and didn't come back." I needed to talk out loud. Let some of the details flow freely. Smitty listened.

"She interviewed me once, you know," I said.

"What was it about?"

"I was lead investigator on a theft case, and we got the conviction. The director of a financial counseling service for the poor had scammed the company and the clients for a couple hundred thousand. Her interview was spot on. She knew how to get to the heart of what harm was done. I was impressed. Genevieve made me look like a hero in the case."

He nodded, but I got the feeling he preferred to see her as a shallow, good-looking shell. It pissed me off. This woman was missing and possibly dead, and he was mentally ogling her. I wondered whether he was the right partner for this unit. I wanted him to be fueled by the injustice of what men did to justify violence against women, not be an active participant in it. I didn't have it in me to take him on right then. *How different was he from the perpetrator we were pursuing?* I wondered. He noticed me assessing him but didn't probe me for an explanation.

Back at the office, Smitty chased down her cell phone records, bank card usage, and bank statements. I contacted the housekeeper, Louise. From our phone conversation, I created a picture in my mind of a Latino woman in her late fifties. She spoke with an accent, exposing that English was likely not the language used at home.

"Has something happened to her?"

"We're really not sure. She hasn't been seen in a couple of days, and her father's concerned. When was the last time you spoke with her?"

"I always clean on Tuesday during the day. She works evenings on the news. Channel 7. Sometimes she is home an hour or so when I begin working, but this week she is gone."

"Did you notice anything different?"

"No, sir. Is Miss Sanders okay?"

"We're just trying to find her right now. Her father let us

in her home to look around this morning. The place was very clean. You do good work."

"Well, thank you, but I didn't have to do much this week. She must have been gone on assignment or something because her house was already very clean. I dusted a bit and put away personal items, but there was not much to do. The trash bins were all empty."

"What sort of personal items were left out?"

"Well, there were some tall black boots in the bathroom. You know the Italian kind with spiked heels and zippers up the back? I put in her closet. Some socks in the bathroom. That sort of thing."

"Are you aware of any enemies Ms. Sanders may have had, or did she mention anything out of the ordinary lately?"

"No. Do you think something happen to her?"

"I hope not. We'll be in touch."

...

Smitty struck out on the bank cards. Nothing had been used since Sunday night. He was drawing up an administrative subpoena for the cell phone provider and social media sites. Chances are she was a Facebooker, Tweeter, and chatter extraordinaire.

"Let's take a ride back up to Woodland. The housekeeper has me curious."

"Yeah? About what?"

"She said the place was already clean, but some boots were lying on the bathroom floor. I want to cross every T and dot every I on this one."

"I didn't see any boots."

"Me, neither. She said she moved them."

At the house, we went upstairs to Genevieve's massive master closet. I quickly spotted the Italian stompers and bagged them up.

"I'm feeling the need for some fine dining. You up for a Coney?" Smitty asked.

"I don't eat that crap, but I'll break my rule if you promise not to stink up the car later."

"Who me? Let's go get some dogs."

Rounding Up the Troops
Chapter 4

Over coney's and a gyro, we processed what we knew so far. If the house was the abduction site, the perp cleaned up. He was either sloppy by leaving items out, or he was deliberately leading us off track. She was missing, and I was getting a bad feeling about her still being among the living. The chances of an abductor keeping her alive beyond twenty-four hours were slim, and after forty-eight hours, the odds got even worse. There was no ransom note, and she had been stalked prior to her abduction.

As we continued to process the case, Smitty's eyes began to glaze over. I wondered if he didn't have some PTSD. He was bound to have wounds from losing his wife and from combat. He caught me looking at him.

"You okay?" I inquired.

"Let me ask you something, man."

"What," I asked, feeling like he was asking me a question to avoid me asking him one.

"You know, I'm pretty good at reading nonverbal behavior."

"Yeah?"

"The way I figure it, you lost that thing one time," he said, motioning toward my gun.

"How's that?" I said, touching my gun to be sure it was well rested in my holster.

"It's either that or you have a heavy petting relationship with it. I've been with you only a few hours, and you've checked it a hundred times. Every room you walked into at that mansion, you checked it before you breached the door. We go up to Woodland, and you're checking it again and again. I'm ordering up my delicacy here, and you're groping it yet again."

"Whatever."

"It's a fact, man. You either have a full-fledged bro-mance going with that thing, or you lost it once." The fact was, I had, but I sure as hell wasn't telling him about it.

Early in my career, I left the damn thing in a gun locker at the jail. We have to lock up our weapons before they'll let us in. I put it in the gun locker to run in and do a quick interview. When I left, I spaced it and drove off. About an hour later, I realized it was gone and had a sick feeling like I'd never experienced. One other time, I stopped at a friend's house to take a dump. I set my gun on the toilet tank and once again drove off without it. In both cases, I made a nonstop flight to recover it. No harm, no foul.

But ever since then, I've had a recurring dream that a dirt bag pulls a gun on me, and I reach for mine to end his quest— only to discover that my holster is empty. The dream always ends before I learn what happens next. The shit of it is, I've had the same dream hundreds of times. I wondered internally if Smitty wasn't the only one who had a case of PTSD.

"I've got no issues other than a deep respect for the thing that has saved my ass and will save it again." *Well, that sounded pretty good. Almost believable.* "So, anyway, before you shared your fetish theory, I was asking you if you were all right."

"Good as gold," he said with a quick smile.

"Really?"

"Good enough for government work. As a public servant, I mean." He winked. I felt the stab of anger as most public servants would. We worked hard for little pay and less thanks.

I nodded, hoping he meant it as a joke. "I'm just saying that I'm here for you, you know?"

He snapped back at me with a fierceness that caught me off guard. "Leave me alone, okay?"

I shot my hands up and backed up a step. He stormed off to the bathroom, leaving me sitting there with the feeling that my partner was a ticking time bomb. When he came out, he was calm and apologized. We both knew we couldn't un-ring that bell. This was one angry, perhaps hostile guy in a nice suit. The honeymoon stage of our partnership was over. I just hoped his detective skills and electronics know-how were enough for me to see past what lay just beneath the surface.

I worried what would happen if we ever really got into it. My name and reputation for hitting first is not a skill. It's a reaction you learn to live with. Two hotheads in our unit would be one too many, and the list of quirks (that were not merely annoying but potentially deadly) in my partner were stacking up.

We rode back to headquarters in silence. He didn't offer me coffee, and I didn't offer him any, either. I made a conscious effort not to touch my gun. Once we settled into our desks, we couldn't avoid each other.

Channel 7 News was on in the background. They broke the story of Genevieve Sanders gone missing.

I sat up in my chair. "Turn that up!"

I listened as they showed footage of Sanders in a variety of scenarios. The newly appointed fill-in anchor even shed a tear and paused in her report to regain her composure.

"Holy shit. Here we go. Now the community is going to freak." They made the story one of concern for their friend and colleague and ended it asking anyone with information to call 911.

"What's our next move, boss?" Smitty raised his eyebrows.

"We're seriously understaffed on this. She's a high-profile TV personality, at least for Duluth anyway. Now the community knows, and there'll be panic and a demand for action. Panic breeds discontent, and the pressure is coming our way. She's missing, and from the look of the house, something that 'needed cleaning up after' happened there. This is not good. We have to bring in everyone we can. Start an all-out canvass of that neighborhood. This thing is going to be all over the media, and we need to stay ahead of it." Smitty nodded agreement.

"I'll ask the lieutenant to call in all of his favors," I continued, "and get a group of cops working on this. We need to search the parks and streams in and around Woodland. See if we can have a couple of search dogs work the area." He nodded again.

Lieutenant Gerard agreed with my assessment that this was time sensitive. It was shaping up to be a political nightmare for him because of Sanders' status as a popular television personality. He pulled several men in from off duty and other shifts and put a request out to the Sheriff's office, as well as to the Hermantown, Proctor, Fond-Du-Lac, and Lake County departments. I asked Smitty to assemble the crew in our shift change room and start getting a plan together to organize the walk and talks. I needed to take another run at her house and interview some neighbors. "You up for it?" I probed.

"Got it!" He didn't look me in the eyes.

While Smitty was developing the canvassing assignments, I raced back to the house and ran through the bedroom one more time with a fine-toothed comb. I had a sixth sense that the snatcher had been in the room. *Had he been here? Did I miss something?* An evil and cold vibe edged its way into my consciousness.

Thirty officers awaited my return, and because most of them were men, the place smelled like a locker room. I took a moment to center myself and compose my thoughts before addressing the troops. Smitty had projected a map of the Woodland neighborhood onto a smart board in the turnout room. I laid out a plan for two canine units to start at the house to see if they reacted to her scent. I assigned four teams to do a canvass of the neighborhood. We used the tactical channel on the radios, and I made it clear that any sensitive information needed to be relayed to me by cell phone. I was certain the hobby cops and reporters were monitoring radio traffic.

We spent the rest of the afternoon and late into the evening knocking on doors. The canine teams had alerted at the house and tracked the victim's scent to the street out in front of the house. They had since begun searching the nearby creek and trail systems.

Our forty-eight hours to get a solid lead was fast evaporating, and I felt the time ticking away. Georgia would understand the late night, and I assume, expect it. All those hours gone, and we had turned up only that Genevieve was a workaholic who mostly socialized with other work people. She attended the occasional neighborhood function but never brought a steady boyfriend. She was pleasant, a little distant, and always dressed to the nines. I met the eleven-to-seven overnight shift and alerted them to our efforts. Our smart board reflected that her immediate neighborhood was nearly searched. I would send whatever crew we got tomorrow out for a second round—hitting neighbors who weren't home and checking whether anyone might have remembered something they forgot to mention in the first meeting.

The data releases from the subpoenas were expected by mid-morning the following day. Smitty and I parted ways with a plan to interview Genevieve's coworkers at News 7 first thing in the morning. I vowed to get some sleep because until this case is finished, there wouldn't be much chance for more.

Creepy

Chapter 5

When I got home, I told Georgia about my interaction with Smitty—the part about him being a loose cannon, not the part about him calling me on my gun-touching habit. She listened closely as she put leftover dinner on a plate for me and then asked, "Want my opinion?"

"Of course." I had a profound respect for Georgia's take on people. She had proven me wrong on a number of occasions.

"The guy is creepy."

"Is that your clinical assessment?"

"Creepy."

"Creepy how?" I probed.

"Like creepy guy creepy. Like I wouldn't trust him alone with my best friend creepy."

"Stalker creepy?" I turned over a rock.

"I'm not sure about that. More like predatory creepy toward women. I lay odds ten to one he will hit on me in some subtle way just because you're his partner."

"Let him try," I said.

"It'll happen. When it does, I'll give you the nod. That doesn't mean you have to take care of anything, though. I take care of myself."

"Was he creepy when his wife was alive or after she died?"

"Both."

"When have you seen him lately?"

"I went to watch Jean play softball last week, and he was there. He wasn't your partner then." She turned her earring, a tell that she was nervous.

"Was he creepy then?"

"He was to Jean. He didn't even ask her out. It was more territorial…looking at her too closely, getting too close to her. She asked me if I noticed. I hadn't, but I was caught up in girl talk."

"Do you think he could hurt someone?"

"Who knows?" She shook her head. "This isn't really my area. I just know creepy when I see it. I'm looking for who to steer clear of."

"Wow, why didn't you say anything earlier?"

"I wanted you to form an open-minded opinion of him. Maybe he's not creepy toward guys. Some guys are like that."

Great, I have a creepy partner, I thought to myself. *Well, what's the worst that can happen? I don't invite him to the usual partner stuff. I have to act like a friggin' guard dog around Georgia's friends.* Not to mention, he would probably never understand that the primary driver of men's violence is their belief that women are "less than." Objects to be used or controlled. That thought pissed me off. Georgia saw me mulling things over and put my pesto chicken with rice in the microwave. *Good. It might half make up for the garbage I had for lunch. While I respect Smitty's service in the military, and computer skills, it doesn't compensate for the fact that he's a creep with women. Gotta keep my eye on this guy.*

Channel 7

Chapter 6

I sent the morning crew of about twenty officers out to re-canvass the Woodland neighborhood and continue searching nearby parks. Duluth is a city built into a steep hillside. A dozen or so creeks and rivers wind their way down that hill from higher ground into Lake Superior. Numerous hiking trails and parks were designed to take advantage of the creeks and rivers, and a large and complicated hiking/cross country ski trail system veins its way through the creeks and parks. While beautiful for the residents and visitors, the urban landscape is a cops' nightmare when someone goes missing. Duluth's proportion of wooded area far surpasses that of most other similarly sized cities in the country, and the Woodland neighborhood was no exception.

Some of the officers were called in, and some came in

voluntarily because they knew we'd need help. I thanked them profusely and reminded them that we were still within the critical first hours of the case. It was important to chase this trail before it got cold.

The creepy thing was on my mind as I met Smitty at Channel 7. I tried to act like I wasn't watching him and probably compensated by being too nice. Either way, we were off balance, and this wasn't good for police work. We needed to tune out all of the other shit and focus on the investigation.

The station manager wasn't Sanders' direct supervisor, but we thought we'd work our way down. Getting his cooperation would help move things a lot quicker with the staff. I led him through the routine questions we were using. Was she seeing anyone? Did she have any scorned boyfriends? Financial trouble? Health problems? Problems with family, friends… Nothing stood out. He pulled the entire news team together as soon as the morning broadcast was done and asked everyone to fully cooperate. We droned through all the staff, asking all of the same questions without uncovering anything new—until we came to Genevieve's makeup artist.

Dean Jones was a veritable wealth of information. He had become her confidant. It took some prying to get him to open up, but when we made him realize that the clock was ticking and he might be our only chance of finding her alive, he opened wide.

"Gen was terrified of someone. She was jumpy all the time. She gave me the flowers he had delivered here. They creeped her out." Jones was originally from South Africa, and he spoke with a British accent and an obvious gay flair.

"What about it creeped her out so much? I need you to be as specific as you can be." I nudged him for details, conscious that I was adjusting my gun again. I wondered if it was alarming to witnesses. He didn't seem to notice my gun, but he did seem to be checking me out.

What is it about me that attracts gay men? One of these days, I'll find the nerve to ask one of them. I was conscious about how this interaction would play out with my new partner.

"The thing that rather spooked her was the news clips edited together. She said it was a professional job. It was almost like it came from our studio."

"Do you have reason to believe it came from inside the studio?"

"I can't imagine so. The people around here are mostly boring. I can't think of anyone who would have enough oomph to be so persistent."

I had to agree with him. The employees we talked with seemed to be shallow and vain. I couldn't imagine any one of them looking beyond themselves too much.

"So Genevieve didn't have any spurned lovers or budding love interests here?"

"Not a one. In fact, Gen didn't want to date at all. Not that she lacked for callers. You know how it is for celebrities, even the local ones. People think that they know you because they see your face every day."

"Did she tell you who she thought it might be?"

"We chatted about it. We even looked through her Facebook friends list to see if she had a bad vibe about anyone. She didn't have a clue." He shrugged and sank down in his chair. "I wish I could be of more assistance. Let me know if there is anything I can do. Really."

"Tell me more about her Facebook friends. Did she regularly communicate with anyone?"

"Everyone! Christ, she must have twenty-five hundred friends." He held up his fingers in quotes when he said *friends.* "She'd accept anyone who requested. Obviously, the vast majority weren't really friends, but it's a social media site, and she used it to the fullest. She posted all the time in the 'what's on your mind?' section and 'checked in' at locations she visited throughout her day. That's how I knew something was wrong. She rarely went several hours without posting something."

Smitty didn't interrupt at all during the whole interview. He kept tinkering with the studio equipment and looking like he wasn't paying attention. It was well beyond noon when we wrapped up. Once in the car, I looked to him for his take on the encounter.

"Faggot," he said without reservation.

"Other impressions?" I wasn't going to feed into his little rant.

"I just gave you one," he said.

"I mean about Genevieve's stalker. The case."

"I'd take a closer look at that guy to start with. He's all concerned about her, but that whole business is cutthroat. Everybody's vying for attention, and she had it. Even the queer guy had to be threatened by that. He specializes in makeup and hair, but he clearly has access to the high-end video gear at the station. Maybe one of this queer dude's ex-lovers, and they all have them, showed an interest in Genevieve. He'd have a clear but twisted motive."

When I didn't respond, either positively or negatively, he added, "The fact that she was a Facebook freak may help us or hurt us."

"What do you mean?"

"Well, the woman has thousands of friends that she checks in with all day. Wouldn't you think these television people would want some privacy when they're off duty? Why would you announce your location everywhere you went?"

I thought about the prospect of interviewing twenty-five

hundred people and must have looked floored. "How can we narrow it down?"

"That's not even scratching the surface. If one of her friends 'likes' a posting of hers, all their friends can now see the post, too. It could go on forever."

"So how might her Facebook account help?"

"I'm hoping she posted comments or chats about being weirded-out by someone. If she told her father, she may have told her friends. The best news is, she left an electronic record of her whereabouts. I may be able to data-wrangle enough information to know where she was or who she was with the day she was grabbed. I'm still betting on the faggot, though."

"Data-wrangle? You make that shit up?"

The smirk was back. "No, but if the shit's out there, I'm on it. I'm as determined to get this as that guy was to get you."

I wanted to point out to Smitty that his homophobia probably stemmed from his misogyny and wondered if he placed gay men above or below women on his hierarchy. I left it for another day. I had neither the energy nor the time to give any attention to his stupidity. *I wonder how all of his crap will affect his ability to follow facts and leads to successfully solve the case.*

I started the car and pulled out of the Channel 7 parking lot aiming us towards headquarters. The social media thing was intriguing.

Not a Creep?

Chapter 7

As we started up the hill toward headquarters, the radio speaker snapped us both from our individual thoughts. We heard the sound of a cop screaming into his radio while in a foot pursuit. It was Sergeant Roe chasing a guy who had just snatched a purse. They were in the skywalks, a system of elevated walkways we all knew well; some from working the beat and others from learning to stay out of the cold all winter. Roe shouted out store names as he passed them like he was giving his location on a named or numbered street: "We're passing Nieman's and headed up north toward Subway." He gasped, trying to catch his breath while sprinting through the crowded skywalk.

"Let me out," Smith demanded.

"No. We're on a murder case. Time is sensitive."

Smitty opened the door anyway and was about to jump out. I stopped abruptly, and he exited the car like a canine released to bite on a fleeing felon. Smitty pulled open the doors of the News Tribune, and I saw him run up the stairs three or four at a time until he disappeared into the skywalk system. I reviewed the map in my head of the skywalk maze. It pissed me off that Smitty had ignored my directive, but I wasn't about to not back up my partner. It's what we do.

I wanted to head them off and be a fresh set of legs, but which way would this guy run? He could head up toward the projects, east to the Fitgers' complex, west to the hotels, or south to the Lakewalk. Miles of tangled skywalks above the streets were designed to link shoppers and patients to their destinations in minus-thirty-degree weather. Roe gave regular updates, and I weaved through the streets below, trying to anticipate the next change in course. As I rounded the corner at Second Avenue, I looked up and saw the perp through the glass running west with Roe in full uniform right on his heels. Roe is young and fit, but police equipment is not conducive to distance running. The tools of the trade make you feel like you've brought a one-ton service truck to a road race. I plotted my course to head them off a block west. Then I saw Smitty sprinting across the glass-enclosed hallway above. He was cruising and closing the gap.

I took a gamble and went two blocks west instead of one, bashed the new Impala over a curb, and left her idling on the sidewalk as I headed up the stairs at the Radisson. When I reached the skywalk level, I turned east, hoping to see the trio headed right for me. My plan was to melt into the crowd until the precise moment when the purse-snatcher arrived. I would step out in front of him like a freight train. It would be a union he would not soon forget.

No one was in the corridor. This told me that bystanders

must have moved east to see what was happening. People always stop to gawk at police action. No matter how ugly or mundane, people just can't resist. I couldn't, either. I rounded the corner into the next block segment. There was a crowd, all right. Roe was standing against the glass, bent over with his hands on his knees, trying to gather oxygen and trying not to puke. Smitty finished applying the cuffs to the runner on the ground as I slid up.

The purse snatcher was a young punk in his early twenties wearing low-riding jeans with a blue bandanna tied on like a tail, a blue T-shirt, and a flat-brimmed blue hat cocked to the left. The kid was sweaty, and I could hear him pant in near unison with Roe. Smitty still looked good in his suit as he patted the kid down for weapons. He was calm, cool, and collected. He wasn't overly aggressive and used his decent looks and confident demeanor to calm the crowd. Smitty flashed his badge, smiled subtly, and encouraged people to move along. Smitty and I escorted the young man to our car while Roe headed back to where he'd seen the kid dump the purse. Roe asked us to locate the victim near Transit Central and have her positively ID our catch. Smitty escorted the cuffed punk through the skywalk back toward the Radisson. There was no conversation.

When we arrived at Transit Central, I stayed in the car with the kid and read him his rights. Smitty approached the victim, who was standing with a downtown clean-team person on the boulevard. The kid told me to fuckoff. He wasn't very talkative after that. With his hands behind his back in cuffs, he couldn't make the adjustment to his hat that he desperately wanted to make. I had turned it to the right. Everything about him was situated in a manner to orient to the left. His tied-on tail, his baggy pants, even his lean was to the left. The left and blue screamed Crip. Gang dynamics are everywhere in America and Duluth was no exception. This kid was a gang member who was now displaying his attire to the right, thanks to me. He didn't want anyone to see him, especially not a rival banger from the Bloods who represent to the right. He was squirming, trying to get the hat turned back, when Smitty and the woman walked up to the side of our car. I stepped out.

"That's him." The woman in her late seventies said.."What the hell is the world coming to? Excuse my language, sonny."

"Are you absolutely certain?" Smitty asked.

"Without a doubt in the world. A woman can't go anywhere anymore without having to worry about some kid who can't even figure out how to pull his pants up. For the love of God." She began to cry and held a handkerchief over her mouth.

"The world is not a bad place, ma'am." Smitty placed his arm around her shoulder from the side. "Kids have been making bad choices for years. They need direction and support. We all want to be cared about, be recognized for our achievements, and feel like we belong. Somehow this gang stuff has filled that need for some kids. We need to work together as a community to fulfill their needs in a positive way, to be role models and help them find a better path. The gangs are just a bunch of kids who need to belong. They are quite violent though. These kids pay a high price for belonging.

What Smitty said hit me hard, and I got lost in his speech. It was damned good stuff, and there was no sign of the creepy guy Georgia had warned me about.

Several minutes later, the woman had regained her control and was reunited with her purse. A beat car took the kid to the juvenile detention center, and we headed to the office to write our supplements.

"That felt great." Smitty checked his appearance in the visor mirror.

"Yeah?"

"Yeah. I mean, we made a difference. If that kid had gotten away, you know he would have done it again and maybe hurt somebody. We were in the right place at the right time for me to catch up to Roe and the kid. Roe was about done."

"I was impressed," I said, but thought that we can't really afford the time. Our vic's clock is ticking. We're losing the battle and losing our chance to find her alive.

"With Roe?"

"Roe was good, but holy shit, you can move! I was looking up from street level and saw a frickin' gazelle run by in a Don Johnson suit."

"Roe and the punk cleared the traffic."

"Yeah, but you were cruising. They say the average criminal is twenty-three years old and in good physical shape. When I was a rookie, I was twenty-three and in good shape, too. Now, the average criminal is still twenty-three and in good shape." We both looked at the beer gut Georgia gives me hell about. "Screw you, Coney boy." I gave him a playful shove and said, "You should think about juvenile when this case wraps up. You have some good skills there."

"As opposed to here?" He smirked.

When we finished our reports, I spent a few more hours going over everything again, and Smitty dove into the recently arrived PDFs from Facebook. I waded through Sanders' electronic banking records and email correspondence. I sent Smitty up to our cube to continue his wrangling while I debriefed the shift of canvassers.

The ground search and canvass had turned up zip. A late-model dark sedan had been parked in the area, but the description was so vague it was useless. I checked in quickly with Smitty, who was knee-deep in records.

"Nothing yet, but there's a lot here."

"Can I help?"

"No. I'm trying to sort it into piles for us to look at. If I find something promising, I'll call you. I want to put this into a timeline of what we have and what the PI for old man Sanders learned. I'll brief you in the morning."

Unwind

Chapter 8

When I arrived home, Georgia wasn't there yet. She was still at karate, but she'd be home soon. Even though it was after eight and I was exhausted, it was my night to cook. As was my habit, I struggled to create a menu that didn't come from a box. I settled on omelets. Thinking of my gut and the footrace today, I dug out spinach, garlic, and goat cheese. If the guys knew I was eating goat cheese, let alone cooking with it, they would give me a lot of ribbing.

"Hey, babe," Georgia said, startling me from assessing my gut in the full-length mirror in the hall. "What's up?"

"Hello to you, too. You look fired up."

"Yeah. I had a great workout and did some sparring with a new girl, Heather, who's a black belt from Iowa. She's a veterinarian, just certified, and she did Taekwondo all through school to stay fit and burn off the study stress. She has about the same reach as I do, and she doesn't hold back. She's tough as hell and focused. I had a blast. She just rented an apartment down in Congdon and started working at the clinic in Lester Park. We really hit it off. Maybe we should have her over some time."

"Maybe we could all practice downstairs," I said as I hugged her and ran two fingers down her spine toward her spandex shorts.

"Don't you ever think of anything else?" She shoved me away. "What's for dinner? Smells decent."

"Gourmet omelets." I got the look. "No—actually something healthy. Give it a chance."

"Let me wash up. I'll be right down."

We sat at the island and sipped some wine with our eggs.

"Smitty continued to intrigue me today. He's a jerk one minute being homophobic, and then he impresses me. I saw a side of him today I haven't seen before. Make that a couple sides." I reached for the salt, earning a frown from Georgia. "He got kind of pissy when I asked him how he was really doing. He looked at me like I was Doctor Phil trying to do an intervention or something. I may have approached it wrong, but he wasn't ready to let me get a glimpse of what's going on with him. Then we had a little excitement this afternoon, and he shined."

I told her about the foot chase and the way Smitty ran like a gazelle and caught the much younger thief. "What was most impressive was the way he handled himself. He was calm and collected at the end of the chase. He wasn't like a lot of cops who are amped up, eager to show a little street justice. He treated the kid with respect and calmed the crowd like a pro."

"Did he woo any women who happened to be bystanders?"

"No. Seriously. He was even better with a grandma who

had her purse stolen. He showed compassion for her and empathy. He tried to get her to understand where the kid might be coming from and what we might be able to do as a community. It was really good. You can't train that into a person. I was impressed. I have to figure out what guides and motivates him. If I can keep him focused and on track, we might be able to fight crime

"Yeah, I know. Wearing the tights of justice."

"Exactly."

"Good to hear, but I still think I already know what guides and motivates him—his manhood. Worse yet, he's a power monger."

"How's the omelet?"

"Not bad."

"See. Good things can happen when you give them a chance. I'm giving Smitty a chance. If I can channel his energy and passion and tap into his technical knowledge, we may be able to do great things."

"Okay, Dr. Freud."

"What? I'm not above figuring this out. After all, I'm an 'investigator.'" I laughed.

"Good luck, but remember, I'm not above saying I told you so."

"Been there."

"Hey, any progress on Genevieve Sanders?"

"We're pounding it, but it's tough. We spent half the day at the TV station. I get the feeling those people are like vultures. She had a ton of Facebook friends, but nobody really seemed to know her except her makeup dude. It was like business as usual. Some new reporter has assumed Sanders' role as anchor, and the sub didn't appear to be the grieving friend she was on TV. What a strange occupation. They aren't paid squat. I guess they're in it for the fame and trying to make it big."

"That's what it's all about."

"Yeah, I guess so. I need to spend some time looking over my case notes tonight. The clock is ticking, and I'm not sure where to go next. Smitty's pouring over tons of Facebook data. This girl's notoriety really makes it difficult. People don't know her, but they think they do. Any number of freaks with a personality disorder could be fixated on her and have a fantasy that they are destined to be together. She's on every night, in our living rooms—and bedrooms. She's on billboards and in magazine and print ads. She does all these personal appearances. She's let people into her life through social media, or at least a persona of her real life. I just wonder if her stalker has developed some ownership tendencies. Maybe he saw her at an event, and she didn't extend the recognition to him he'd dreamed up in his head. Maybe he's trying harder to get noticed or to get them together; probably keep them together in his mind. Or maybe he's angry that she blew him off. Maybe he perceives it as if Sanders dumped him even though there was really nothing to end."

"Sounds like you need some time. I'll leave you alone to your pondering. I'm going to bed now, hon, so when you come up, keep it stealthy."

"All right, babe. Love you." I settled into my chair after pouring another glass of wine. I had some serious thinking to do. In the morning I'd regret the wine, but hell, it wasn't morning yet.

Gruesome

Chapter 9

I must have dozed off because I woke to my cell phone blaring my 911 signal at 2a.m. It was the communications center. Genevieve Sanders had turned up. Dead. They wouldn't give me details over the phone, just that she was found in the Rose Garden. I asked if Smitty had been notified. They told me he hadn't answered, and they were trying to page him. I grabbed a quick shower, knowing I'd be at it a while. I started working on my plan in the shower. I grabbed a reheated cup of coffee and some peanut butter toast to erase any remnants of the wine. Once in the car, I advised communications I was en route. They hadn't heard from Smitty, but they would continue to try. I proceeded to the Rose Garden.

It was a cool forty-five degree night, and the dew hung in the air and on each rosebud as I made my way over to the decorative vine-draped arch in the center of the garden, which was a healthy walk from the road and the business of the nearby city. I had dreamt of marrying Georgia under this arch as we watched two of our friends tie the knot in this very spot. It was as close as I had come to a proposal. The only thing holding me back was a deep-seated fear that she was too good for me, and that because of my job, I was too unavailable. The setting was beautiful, with Lake Superior as a backdrop and surrounded by roses. Bustling by day, the park was sleeping and desolate at night.

My breathing picked up as I approached, and my breath produced little puffs from the cold. I had to stop to take it all in. Rose petals led a pathway to her. Genevieve Sanders stood posed in a wedding dress with no groom. Made up, hair done, and standing where the bride would stand, she was clearly dead. Her wrists and ankles bore the distinctive marks of having been tied or cuffed, but how was she still standing? Her right hand was poised over her heart. I must have been staring open-mouthed because a uniformed officer came up to me from the side.

"She's on a mannequin stand, sir."

"And the hand?"

"Wired."

"What's the safest way to approach?" I needed to get closer without disturbing any evidence.

He handed me booties to slide over my shoes and guided me to a spot ten feet from the body. Her hair was styled, but clearly not by her regular hairdresser, and the poorly applied makeup barely covered the corpse's pallor. No bruising was visible, but she had a look of sheer terror on her face. I wondered if her killer's fantasy was wrecked by that look.

"Quite the wedding, eh?" asked Larsen, the evidence man from ID.

His question was impossible to answer, so I took a more professional approach. "Do we know time of death yet?"

"Still waiting for the coroner."

"Any guess?"

"Hard to tell with the makeup. Midnight to 3 a.m.? Looks like she's in full rigor. I'm guessing she died elsewhere and was posed here. I shot the overalls and am searching for trace stuff. I'd like to wait for daylight to take more photos. I'm thinking we'll garage her after we collect the trace evidence on the perimeter."

The techs had a new trick of using a garage in a box. They set up metal poles and covered their crime scene with the thick, heavy tarp included in a twenty-by-thirty foot kit. Nothing was disturbed, and it kept the gawkers at bay. Without it, seeing this bride would be hard on the morning joggers.

"A garage wedding in the park. What kind of a person would do something like this?"

I asked the question rhetorically, but Kent seemed to take it seriously. "Determining the kind of person is a profiler's job or a detective's. Mine is to turn over every piece of evidence in this crime scene."

I was used to unusual comments from Kent, but he was superlative in his work. This was likely the case of my career, and I needed him and everyone else on point. Smitty was nowhere in sight. Not a good start to the day.

"I see the coroner just pulled up." Kent turned to meet her.

"I'm sure we'll have some facts soon," I said, hoping that was true. I really needed to move my own thinking along. The clock was ticking, and every second mattered. While I helped with the evidence collection, I tried furiously to figure out what I was dealing with.

I've got to get inside this guy's head. I have a feeling he's just getting started. Damn.

I shivered involuntarily, wondering if we weren't in over our heads. I settled on the conclusion that we definitely were. I pictured Genevieve doing the news and hanging around home. I needed to tap into her humanity to fuel my confidence that I could catch the perpetrator. The only motivation for doing this kind of work had to be a passion for putting things right. Not as right as they were before the gruesome murder, but righter when the bad guy sees a jail cell.

The crime scene technicians and I spent the next several hours bagging and tagging the apparatus the killer had used as well as items of litter in the vicinity of the body, and then we brought it back to the lab. The coroner processed the body and packaged it for the morgue. The lab work would take time. Time we didn't have. I was so wrapped up in the scene that I completely forgot about Smitty until he called me at 0830.

"Boss. I just woke up. I see you and the comm. center have been burning up my phone."

"No shit. The news star woke up dead in the Rose Garden. I've been working this all night with the booger-eaters from ID and the coroner's office. Where the fuck have you been?"

"It's this damn Ambien. I can't sleep without it, but I swear I'd sleep through my own house fire. I seriously have to be horizontal before I even take it, and then I'm out for eight hours."

"Whatever. Take a 'wake the hell up' pill and meet me at the Duluth Grill—not inside, but in the parking lot. You're not going to believe this."

I grabbed a double sausage breakfast sandwich to go and waited in my car in the back corner of the lot for Smitty. Georgia would kill me if she knew I was eating a twelve-hundred calorie heart attack on a plate. I could almost hear my arteries slamming shut as Smitty pulled up door to door.

"Dude. I really am sorry."

"Spare me, Sleeping Beauty. The crime scene was like nothing I've ever seen."

"Gory?" he said, eating an apple and drinking coffee from a Quick Mart styro cup.

"Not gory—eerie. This death scene was way the hell out there." I've seen plenty of death, but I always distanced myself from it. I know the person who occupied the body meant something to somebody, but I don't get wrapped up in that. I don't go to funerals of victims like some guys do because I want to maintain my distance from the human element. I don't want to see people grieve or celebrate what a great person the deceased was. I focus on the vehicle, look for evidence and clues, and try to stay objective with no emotion. The wedding scene flashed in front of my eyes.

"Something was different. As I walked in from London Road, I could see a figure standing in the arch where, you know, people get married. It was a friggin' bride wearing a bridal gown and veil. She held a bouquet of flowers, facing the lake like she was facing her future. Rose petals led the way to her posed body. She even held her hand over her heart in an expression of admiration. I couldn't help but think of old man Sanders and the dreams he must have had for her."

"How did she look?"

"She looked dead. She had a look of horror on her face that I hope the killer took at its full value. He had put crappy makeup on her face, but make no mistake about it, she was dead. And she didn't die peacefully. She died in terror, and it looked like she had a tough time of it. She'd been tied up for days and tortured. The son of a bitch put her through hell."

"Any trace evidence?"

"I hope so, but she appeared to have undergone some cleanup. The scene smelled of bleach about as bad as her place did the day we were there. I'm betting we'll find something. The dress. The shoes. The transport. It's a public place. Someone had to have seen something."

"I don't know. It's pretty secluded at night." Smitty wasn't being too optimistic.

"Not that secluded. It's in the middle of a city." I put my head against the steering wheel. This was draining all of my energy. "Meet me at the morgue!" I drove off with a squeal— partially because I was pissed Smitty wasn't there to help and partially because the human element had a strong hold on me. Like it or not, I was personally involved.

Smitty had a hard time keeping up with me as I drove to the morgue. I took my frustrations about him out in my driving. I knew I was creating a potential hazard on the road, but I just couldn't rein it in.

Dr. Tollefson, or Tollie as we called her, was just cutting into the chest when we arrived. I didn't have a lot of experience at the morgue, and she sensed it. The smell over powered the gum I had popped into my mouth. She asked us to step into her office, taking a break from the autopsy. She was in her mid-thirties, with brown hair and attractive Bambi eyes, wearing light blue scrubs. I couldn't help but notice Smitty puffing out his chest. Christ. I was quickly losing my newly found respect for his character.

"Well, the external told me a lot."

Smitty and I sat eagerly awaiting her findings.

"There was no skin tissue under her fingernails. It's not that she didn't fight. Someone had meticulously cleaned her hands, soaking them in bleach, and then applied fingernail polish to each nail on the inside and outside. I found nothing that connects us to her assailant."

"Nothing anywhere? Or nothing on the nails?" I probed.

"Nothing on her nails or anywhere else for that matter. She

was sexually assaulted, torn vaginally and anally, but again, she was cleaned with bleach and all of her body hair was shaved. Whoever did this went to great lengths to cover his tracks."

"What can you tell us about what happened to her?" I needed something if I was going to prevent the future attacks I suspected were coming.

"I can show you better than tell you." She led us back to the table.

"See these ligature marks." She pointed to Genevieve's wrists and ankles. "It looks like he used nylon rope and flexi-cuffs. The injuries happened over an extended period of time. Days." She looked at me to make sure I followed. "She was dehydrated. I haven't gotten to her stomach contents yet, but I don't expect to see anything there unless the perpetrator ejaculated into her mouth. I may find some DNA in her esophagus or stomach, but the tearing makes me think he used an object."

I flinched when she spoke so casually of the brutality of Genevieve's captivity and assault. She softened. "Look, why don't you leave your cell number, and I'll call you with my results? We have a lot of ground left to cover."

I managed to pull it together enough to ask her about the time of death. Tollie said the liver temp put time of death at roughly midnight.

"What about the veil and dress? There has to be something," I asked desperately. "I think the dress was put on postmortem, so I don't expect to get usable trace from it. I'm no fashion expert, but that thing was custom made, probably decades ago. Someone with money had it designed. Only a couple of shops in the area could have completed an order like that. It most certainly didn't come off a rack." She looked over her cheaters at me. "I'll email you a good picture of the dress."

I got up on shaky feet and walked out to the squad car, where Smitty and I pondered our next move.

"Let's give the doc some time and space. I need to pay a personal visit to Genevieve's father before this goes public. The poor guy. Then I'll start pounding the area shops, and you can check public cameras for any possible footage of the wedding. Pull out all of your techie-stops. I'll get in touch with my feminine side and do some dress shopping. Put some miles on and talk to anyone who may have seen anything. After all, you're well rested with your Ambien-induced eight hours."

"I'm sorry."

"Yes, you are." I gestured for him to leave with a dismissive wave. "Wait, what about that social media?" I shouted after him at the last second.

"There is so frickin' much to look through, but I'm on it. You sniff out the dress."

My next stop was the Sanders mansion in Congdon. The butler didn't utter a word after I announced my name; he just buzzed me in. Mr. Sanders was seated in his study. He stood as I entered, but I motioned for him to sit, taking a chair across the desk from him. His eyes looked tired. I couldn't tell whether he'd heard the news about Genevieve. He sat quietly watching me, letting me initiate the conversation.

"I'm sorry, sir. We found Genevieve, and she…" I hesitated, searching for the right words, knowing there were no right words. "She didn't survive."

He nodded, not as though he had heard from an external source, but as though my words had only confirmed something he already knew. A flash of sadness and then anger lit in his eyes.

"Did she suffer?" he asked.

"Some, I'm afraid, but she was drugged, so I hope that

mitigated a lot of it." I pictured the tortured look on her face, and some of the brutal details intruded into my thoughts. I tried to remain stoic outwardly.

"Was she raped?" he asked, his words faltering through tears.

"She's still at the morgue, and the final test results aren't in, but I'd say it's likely." I couldn't completely whitewash this. The news stations would carry the gruesome details. It was better he heard them from me. He hung his head in his hands and sobbed. "She was my baby. She was so sweet. Oh, my god... My baby."

I knew nothing I would say could soften the news or the mental pictures of his daughter being tortured and raped by a killer, but I had to try. "I'm so sorry for your loss. I'll do everything I can to catch her killer. Not only for Genevieve, but for other potential victims." He didn't seem to hear me. But I kept on talking. I was uncomfortable with his pain.

"I know this is a lot to take in, and you'll have more questions. Please don't hesitate to call me for anything." I slid a card across the desk to him. "My cell phone number is on there, and I'll answer it 24/7." He still wept. I sensed him running through the memories of her childhood in his mind. "Do you have someone to be with you?"

He nodded, and I let myself out quietly. The air was crisp outside. As is common in Duluth, the wind had shifted and now came off the big lake, dropping the temperature by fifteen degrees in a matter of minutes. I felt chilled to the bone and shook off a pang of intuition that my world and the world of my hometown were about to be turned upside down. I thought about Alex and let a few sweet memories of his childhood surface before grabbing my light jacket out of the trunk and making my way downtown.

En route, I called Georgia for support and for advice on

where to find high-end, antique wedding dresses. While I didn't necessarily process the next-of-kin notification with her, just hearing her voice was a comfort to me. She suggested I try the secondhand shops. She also said I should ask the coroner if the victim wore a standard size. If she did, anyone could have ordered the dress online. If not, it would have required custom tailoring. The only bridal shop in town she knew of was on London Road in an old turn-of-the-century mansion called Penelope's.

I retrieved the pictures Tollie had sent me of the dress via email and headed for London Road.

The shop owner could tell when I first stepped through the door that I wasn't there to pick out a gown or to rent a tux. She was a tall redhead with bright green eyes. I showed her my badge and then the pictures. She crossed her arms and shivered as she looked closely at the dress. The old mansion was drafty, and the cold wind was working its way through the windows, doors, and poorly insulated walls.

"It didn't come from here, but I can tell you it's an antique. The buttons are old anyway. The clasps, too. This would be almost impossible to track down. I would assume someone saved it in a cedar trunk. I don't see any damage or fading." She ran her hand over the picture as if to touch the fabric. "Was this from the woman found in the Rose Garden?" She looked into my eyes earnestly. The news had broken.

I nodded.

"Not the wedding she had hoped for." She shuddered. I could see goose bumps on her arms.

I left my card in case she thought of anything else. The folks at the secondhand store didn't recognize the dress but referred me to a website that specialized in antique wedding dresses. I had work to do.

As I walked to my car, I heard my cell ring. The caller ID

read Minnesota Video Relay. Only one person would be calling me via relay, so I picked up: "Alex. What's up, buddy?"

A female operator relayed my sentences to Alex via sign language and interpreted his signed messages to me verbally. "Hello, Dad. I saw a story on TV about a killing in Duluth. What do you know about it? Are you the lead investigator on the case?"

The relay operators have a strict code of confidentiality, but I was less than comfortable revealing anything about the case, especially to a stranger. I started to respond and held my words. "Hey, I really can't talk about it right now. We'll catch up soon, okay?" I waited for his response. The operator simply said: "End of call."

Shit! A few seconds later, I felt my phone shake with an incoming text. It was from Alex. Six words: "You never have time for me." He didn't deserve being blown off, but I would have to pick up the pieces later.

I called Smitty with what I had learned on the dress. He said that he was just about to call me. Another woman had gone missing. I met him at the station.

Serial?

Chapter 10

I felt tense as I met up with Smitty just outside the Lieu's office. The mayor was with Gerard, and they were having one of those discussions where they try to look at ease, but they're screaming internally.

I pulled Smitty aside, interrupting him as he watched me adjust my gun. *Damn. Why did he have to point that out to me? How many other people noticed it? Never mind, all cops adjust their guns,* or so I told myself.

"Know anything?" I asked.

"Not a damn thing. You?" He gestured with his chin.

"If this is related, we've got a serial killer." Something flashed in his eyes. I couldn't tell whether it was fear, anger, or excitement.

"Damn," he said, slumping back against the wall.

"We need help," I said.

"If it's related." He seemed to want it not to be.

We were in deep shit, behind the eight ball, and up the proverbial creek—with no leads. I felt myself slide into wishful thinking about fishing in my concrete honey hole for speeders before I pulled myself together. "Let's get in there and face the music."

I knocked on the door, and through the window, the Lieu motioned silently for us to enter and have a seat. He and Mayor Green were both standing behind the desk.

"Sorry, boss, I need to stand," I said. Smitty stood quietly beside me.

"Have it your way, then." He clasped his hands together and pulled them up to his nose in a clear effort to compose himself. A drip of sweat rolled down his sideburn onto his collar. He started to speak and stopped himself for what seemed like an eternity. The air felt electric. I let the silence hang there. Mayor Green started speaking, and the Lieu cut him off.

"It's Andrea Hotelman." Gerard looked at me.

"Andrea, who works in sex crimes?" I asked in a high-pitched voice. Andrea and I had dated discreetly for about two years, but the crazy demands of our jobs put too much strain on the relationship. We had remained friends. Her beautiful face and easy smile flashed in front of my eyes. "Is she missing or dead?" I had to know.

"Missing."

"How do we know?"

"Her boyfriend reported her missing and said she had been stalked."

"Stalked how, and missing how long?" I fired questions at him as I approached. "Did we know about the stalking?"

Smitty placed a hand on my shoulder, and I realized I needed to ease up on the rapid-fire questions. Everyone in the room must have thought I was on the edge of coming unglued.

"The boyfriend is a probation officer who works in the sex offender unit. He said she went missing the night Ms. Sanders was discovered. He said the stalking had been a recent thing. Flowers at work, things rifled through at her home. Someone even left a rose petal on her desk at work."

"Here? In the station?" I was incredulous. He nodded silently. The mayor stepped forward to gain my attention.

"I don't have to tell you the pressure we're under here. When this hits the news, every woman in town is going to freak. The fact that a police officer was taken is a pretty bold move."

I sat down. This wasn't just any police officer; this was my ex—someone I had a personal history with, yet we had come out the other end as friends. I didn't give a damn about the pressure he was under.

Swallowing hard, I tried to calm myself. We were all on the same team. I needed to be really careful. If the Lieu knew how involved Andrea and I had been, I would be off the case in a heartbeat. The last thing I needed was to be yanked off the case. I stood again.

"In that case, we need more help. If these kidnappings are related, this is a serial offender, and he won't stop with Officer Hotelman as his last victim. Lieu, with your permission, I'd like to assemble a team of at least four more cops. More if we can get them. See if the volunteers we used before can come back. They know the routine now. Let's brief in the conference room in fifteen. We need to get out there while she might still be alive." My pulse pounded, but I stood erect, poised to battle for someone I cared about.

"I'll call them in," the lieutenant said.

I walked into the bathroom down the hall and threw up

until there was nothing left. Any thought of the honey hole was gone. I had to find her alive.

By the time I got to the conference room, Lieu had assembled a team of six officers with two more coming in from the field. I looked around and noticed they were all men. I spoke up.

"This is great, Lieu. Do we have a female cop we can bring in? It might help to have someone on the team who can think about things from that angle. Can we tap into the feds? Maybe get a profiler?" I heard groans in the room, but Lieu nodded and headed out the door to make some calls.

"Okay, guys. Let's get a plan together." They all stood at attention waiting for direction. I assigned teams to interview her boyfriend, family, neighbors, and workmates. After they headed out, Smitty and I stood alone in the room absorbing the silence for a few seconds.

Lieu returned with news.

"Okay, I've got Kennedy coming from the FBI," he said. I briefed him about the plan, and we waited for Kennedy to arrive. She strode in, tall and lean in a dark pantsuit. While she appeared calm on the exterior, her eyes held a spark I recognized as intelligence mixed with a healthy dose of adrenaline. I brought her up to speed as quickly as possible. She interrupted me at times to drill deeper into the details she needed.

When I began talking to her about Andrea, she stopped me. "You know her. How?"

"We're good friends."

She saw right through me. "Can you be objective?"

"Absolutely not. I won't stop until I find her."

"Are you still in love with her?" She watched me intently.

"I love her as a friend."

"Do you have a partner, a girlfriend?" she asked, examining my ring finger.

"Yes." I felt defensive. "We're all friends."

"You may need to be pulled from this thing at some point. Prepare yourself for that." She composed her thoughts before moving on. "Okay, here's what I have so far. The wedding theme is obvious. Maybe too obvious, but it's critical. He got left at the altar, was rejected, or maybe his parents never married. There's something there." She waited for a reaction or comment.

"The location is also significant. There's an emotional connection to the Rose Garden for him. We have to place it under surveillance. We should put women cops under cover in the area. Jogging, walking… you know the drill. Is there a way to hook up a camera? Can you do that?" She looked at me. I looked at Smitty. He nodded, said "I'm on it," and left for the supply room.

"Maybe the head gardener can help us. This is a city garden, right?"

I nodded, pulling out the employee directory and arranging for the gardener to meet us at the Rose Garden.

On the way, Kennedy introduced herself to me properly. Her first name was actually Karen, but she'd grown accustomed to responding to her last name. "It's part of the job, being known by your last name, just like everyone else. I guess it's a compliment."

Kennedy asked me to reenact the posed crime scene for her. Then she had me go through it again, describing it from the perspective of how I felt when I walked up to it.

"This is a cinema for him. He's telling the world a story," she explained.

"At first I was horrified that a woman was posed. Then I got caught up in the whole marriage scene. It made me think about my own possible ceremony. The hopes, dreams, fears… you know." She nodded and listened intently. "Once I drew near, my cop mind wanted to know how he did it. I wanted to figure out how he'd posed her." I nodded toward where she had stood. "Then it became clear to me that she was dead. The serenity and beauty of a wedding scene was desecrated by death and a bad makeup job."

Kennedy stopped me. "Do you think the makeup was intentionally sloppy, or just bad because it was done by an amateur?" she asked.

I took a minute. I hadn't formed a judgment about it. "I think it was intentionally sloppy, but I'm not really sure. I don't have a lot of experience with makeup. It would be hard to make a corpse look good, right?" She nodded.

"Still, it was exaggerated. Like she was made to look tragically overdone. We took plenty of pictures."

When the master gardener arrived at the scene, she shook our hands after removing a well-used glove. The petite woman expressed her sympathy about what had happened to Genevieve. But then she surprised me by her concern for the roses.

"I shudder to think about what they were witness to, what kind of dark energy they absorbed." She looked like she was about to cry. I pulled out pictures of the petals that had been used to lead a pathway to Genevieve, and she confirmed that they were taken from the garden. "In fact, I can show you the exact bush they came from."

We walked over to a bush well away from the wedding area near a bike path that led to the Lakewalk. "They all came from this bush. Right here." She gestured at a bush that looked sparse.

Once the meeting was over, I asked Kennedy for her impressions.

"I think this is someone who is very sensitive, and she found the right calling when she became a gardener. She prefers time with flowers and peaceful contemplation to the company of humans."

"So we can cross her off the suspect list?" I said with a smile.

"She never made it to mine." She returned my smile.

"Do you think roses can feel evil?"

"I think it's likely." This time she didn't smile. "But more important, I think our killer took the petals ahead of time. It explains why the bush was so far from the posing area. He didn't want to be noticed taking them. It means he had been planning this scene before the abduction."

We spent a bit more time at the Rose Garden and on the Lakewalk, taking in details before returning to the office to review photos, catch up with progress on the investigation, and plan for the press release.

Mayor Green joined us to sign off on the draft. Tension radiated from him as he entered the conference room. Chief Campbell accompanied him.

"Tell me we've made some progress," Green said in a commanding tone.

"We're putting everything into this," Gerard said, motioning for the mayor to take a seat.

"I'm sure you are, but what do you have? Who is your suspect?"

"We're interviewing friends, family, setting up surveillance. It takes time."

"We don't have time," Green pushed.

"Agreed," I said.

Chief Campbell jumped in and said, "We have one of the top crews in the country. If we don't have anything yet, we'll get there. Rome wasn't built in a day."

"What do you have now? We have to give the vultures something." Green looked frustrated and weary. He seemed to deflate as he turned toward the window, probably thinking about the fear and frenzy that would follow the announcement of a serial killer preying upon women and even women cops in Duluth.

"We have a good start on a profile," Kennedy spoke up. We all raised our eyebrows, thankful she was taking some of the heat.

"It's likely a white male, twenty-five to forty-five years old, who has significant issues with women. He's been rejected in a way that was publicly humiliating by someone he idealized. Then he later found out that she was flawed or human in a way he didn't expect. He has issues with marriage because of something in his own life or his parents' lives. He is likely socially awkward but intelligent. He will have a past history of stalking women and may have a history of violence against former partners. He may have killed before and gotten away with it. He has significant control issues that will manifest in all areas of his life."

"Is that the press release?" I said to the chief.

"That and the fact that we are working with the FBI and every available resource to apprehend the killer."

"We have to set up a call line that's staffed around the clock," Kennedy said in an even tone. "I'll train the operators about what follow-up questions to ask to weed out the crackpots. We'll get a ton of calls. A lot of guys out there have control issues, especially in their relationships with women.

"We'll provide the call staff with a script of questions. They can type on a form and summarize the answers as they field the calls. We'll filter the responses through two screeners, whom I'll also train. Then I'll read the ones that don't get filtered out."

Green looked pale, but he seemed to take some comfort in our plan. He muttered, "Keep me posted," as he walked out.

Chief Campbell nodded at everyone and said, "Good work.

Keep me posted as well, Randall." If he hadn't been looking right at Lieutenant Gerard, I wouldn't have known who he meant. Somehow the fact that Lieu had a given name jarred me into the realization of just how far down the command chain I served.

Our Finest

Chapter 11

As investigators checked in from the field with updates, Kennedy took their reports. I updated Lieu, who updated the chief, who weighed what he would share with the mayor. It was dark, we'd had a long day, and it wasn't even close to being over. Nothing solid was coming in about Andrea. My heart constricted in my chest as dead end after dead end trickled in over the phone or in person. I paced as I interviewed a helpless young detective named Lyle Anderson.

"Where was she last seen?" I pushed.

"Yesterday at work. Someone saw her at her desk in the morning."

"Where is her field partner?"

"On vacation this week in Aruba, sir."

"Did you verify he went?" I said sharply.

The detective looked like I'd slapped him. "No, sir."

"Look, I'm sorry I'm coming off like an insensitive jerk, but we have to treat everyone as a suspect. Just cross the T's and get back to me." I knew I'd been too harsh. Lyle walked quietly out. I'd had other questions for him, and now it was too late. I needed to get a grip.

I walked to the vending machine and fueled up on a Snickers bar that I washed down with coffee. When I got back to the conference room turned command center, Smitty was waiting for me. He approached me gingerly. Word must have already spread about my mood. "We'll find her."

I took a calming breath. "How goes it with the camera?"

"Excellent. Come over here." He motioned me to a laptop.

The monitor was split into six smaller screens, each showing a different part of the Rose Garden/Lakewalk area. Smitty was as animated as I've ever seen him. "I put up cameras that look like park signs. 'Park closes at 10 p.m.' The camera lenses are embedded in the 0 of 10. They're battery operated, and they have limited night vision capabilities. Look, I can control the brightness from here." He moved a dial on the mouse, and the picture lightened and darkened. Then he moved the mouse, and one of the screens expanded into full view.

"Really nice work, Smitty. Does it record?"

"Not yet. I'm working on that. I have to hook it up to an external hard drive. We don't have one big enough, so I gotta go shopping."

I sent him on his way and then walked through the department in search of Kennedy. I found her set up in a meeting room. She was reading through the tip sheets. She had them in three piles. When she finished one, she looked up. "Nothing promising yet. When I find something, I'll call you." She began reading again.

"What are the piles?"

"Nut case, follow up, and funny."

"Follow up?" I raised my eyebrows in inquiry.

"We need to make sure the caller is legit. Sometimes the perps will insert themselves into the call-in process. They get curious, want to throw us off, or just like to be closer to the madness they're creating."

I grabbed one of the sheets from the pile. I couldn't see anything that raised my curiosity. It was a guy reporting his sister's ex as a stalker. I was glad Kennedy had the patience for this. "So, how do we follow up?"

"We call a second time, and if things don't add up, we send a squad to the house. You'd be surprised at what we find with this process."

"Thanks for all of this," I said, waving my hand over the piles.

"No trouble. You okay?" She pointed her intense eyes at me.

"I will be if we find her." She nodded and went back to her reading.

I took the short hike to our lab, essentially a catacomb-like space in the basement of the law enforcement building. With half windows and high-efficiency bulbs lighting the mostly stainless steel and white surfaces, it had a sterile, medical feel. Larsen was hunched over a microscope in the middle of the lab. He had headphones on, and I had to tap him on the shoulder to get his attention.

"Have you turned up anything useful?" I inquired.

"Useful is a strong term," he said with irritation.

"Do you have anything that can point us to a suspect? Something we can send in for DNA analysis? Blood type? Anything?" I knew my voice had taken on a desperate tone.

"I'm still working on that," he said without elaboration.

"What does that mean?" My tone got a little harsher. I sensed I was on thin ice. I needed his cooperation, but I resented having to pull the facts out of him.

"Look, Striker, why are you here? Everything was contaminated. I mean everything. It's as if he soaked her in bleach. This guy knew what he was doing. I've never seen anything like it. I'm going to have to go over every shred of evidence with a microscope. It's painstakingly slow. Interrupting me is not going to get it done any faster." He put his headphones back on and peered into the microscope.

"Damn," I said to no one.

I wondered if he was right. Looking over everyone's shoulders and breathing down their necks wasn't getting me any closer to solving the case and finding Andrea. My team was a good one. If we could stay united, we might have a chance of catching this lone killer—maybe.

...

I needed to get out of the office. I felt seriously cooped up all of a sudden. I told the lead clerical person to call me if anything came up. Then I got in my cruiser and drove to Canal Park, where I got out and took the Lakewalk a mile to the Rose Garden. I expected to run into officers doing their canvassing and speaking to other walkers, but it was dusk, and I saw very few people.

I found a bench where I had a slight view of Rose Garden central, but it wasn't obvious that I was watching. I pulled out my cell, saw that Georgia had called, and dialed her up.

"What the hell?" she obviously had heard.

"I know. Crazy, right?"

"I was feeling a little edgy already, and then you're butt-dialing me."

"Butt-dialing?"

"Yeah. Unless you meant to call me three times in the last hour and hang up right away."

"Shit. Sorry. I saw that you called me, but I was in a strategy meeting."

"I called your dumb ass back to make sure you were okay."

She was freaked out about Andrea. When something like this hits close to home, it's so much more real. She signed off, sounding a little distant or scared—I couldn't tell which.

As I closed the phone, I noticed movement over by the wedding spot. I pretended to get another call and began talking into the phone as I slowly made my way toward it. A man was kneeling at one side of the circle as if in prayer. While keeping my head down, I continued to talk into the phone, pretending to be arguing with someone. When I got within fifty feet of the man, he bolted upright and took off toward the lake. I radioed dispatch and requested a squad as I tried to keep up with him. He was medium height, medium build, wearing jeans, a blue sweatshirt, and a baseball cap over short dark hair.

By the time I crossed the bridge that led down to the Lake-walk, he was gone. Vanished. I searched several hundred feet in both directions but couldn't get a bead on him. After giving his description and last known location to the units in the area, I gave up, hoping they would spot him.

I walked back up to the Rose Garden wedding circle and went over to the area where the man had been kneeling. A small stone lay on the ground. I took a picture with my phone before picking it up. It was a hand-chiseled gravestone roughly the size of an phone. On one side, the inscription read "Genevieve Sanders 2015"

I rushed back to the station and found Smitty hunkered down over his laptop. "Did you see me in the Rose Garden?"

He nodded yes without speaking. He was concentrating.

"Did you see the guy?"

He nodded yes but continued working, typing furiously. He stopped, stood up, and slammed his fist down. "Damn it." He paced. "I had him on the camera and was this close to having the hard drive set up to record it. I thought I might have a shot of him, but it's gone. Fucking gone. That was him. We had him."

"Tell me about it. I was within fifty feet of him."

"Did you see his face? Get enough for a composite?"

I shook my head. "Too dark." I held up the miniature gravestone. "I gotta run this by Kennedy. I'm sure this means something for the profile." He gave me a look that clearly implied he thought profiling was bullshit.

It suddenly occurred to me that I had no way of knowing if Smitty was really in the office watching me on camera when I ran across the perp in the Rose Garden. He got here awfully fast, and something seemed strange about him. I had my doubts about him as a partner, but I couldn't quite believe that he might actually be the killer. The one thing I didn't doubt was that I wanted more oversight on him. I grabbed the first officer I spotted and asked him, "Who's our best technology guy?"

"Smitty."

"Besides him."

"Me, I think," he said, while jutting his hand out. "Corey Groves."

"What are your qualifications?" I probed.

"I was a programmer in a former life, and I live to game." He brightened. He was in his late twenties with some acne still present. "I mean, after living to be a cop, I live to game."

"Sounds like you will be exactly what I need. What detail are you assigned to?" It seemed to take forever for him to respond, so I pushed him. "On this case, what is your assignment?"

"I'm not on this case, sir. I was just passing through. I'm assigned to the computer lab."

"Who is your supervisor?"

"Lieutenant Dane."

"You're now reassigned. I'll let him know. Your job is to be Smitty's personal assistant. You're to stick to him like glue. Drive him to work, home, get him coffee, do whatever he needs, but I want you where he is at all times. Got it?"

His eyebrows shot straight up, and he sported a huge grin.

"Thank you, sir. I won't let you down." He strode over to Smitty with purpose. I figured I'd better go with him. I would need to explain this to Smitty in a way that made it look like support rather than oversight. I suspected he would rather enjoy having a personal assistant.

"Hey, Smitty, I got you some technical help."

"Really?" he said sarcastically. "Don't you think I'm competent enough?"

"We need all the help we can get." Smitty had claimed to be good at reading nonverbals, and maybe he was.

"You want to help, get out there and interview some suspects," he growled. "I'm in here staring at computers so long that my eyes hurt, busting my ass on the technical side, and you're going for a walk on the Lakewalk. What the hell? How could you not catch that guy? You should be running in your off time, not leisurely walking. Maybe you could start by running down to Channel 7 and interrogating the fag again. Be sure to get a look at his hindquarters to see if it's a match for the killer who just outran you."

"Look, I'm working all suspects and all leads," I said. Arguing wasn't helping either of us. He was pissed off that I had assigned someone to "Help him."

"I'll take your assistant, but get out of my face."

I left a voicemail for Dane and then drove to the station where I found Kennedy lording over her three piles. She looked up. "Nothing yet, Grasshopper. You have to be patient."

"No, I have something for you." That made her eyes perk up. I was aware that I shifted my feet and checked my damn gun. It pissed me off that Smitty had made me self-conscious not only about the gun but also about my fitness. At the same time, this was the first lead we had, and it was all I could do not to run in place. "We almost had him. I found him praying at a makeshift grave. He'd made a headstone for Genevieve."

She considered this for a minute, walked a few paces herself, then said, "Okay, so we know he is religious and not a sociopath, and the fact he laid down a headstone implies he is capable of empathy. She paused thoughtfully again. "It means either he knew her well before the abduction, or his stalking led to a prolonged fantasy of a relationship. He believed the wedding would have united them in eternity, but something went wrong. Now he's grieving the loss. He may have had to kill her because she wouldn't submit to his wishes, or she fought him."

I sat down. This wasn't what I had hoped. I had pretty much surmised all of that except the knowledge that he wasn't a sociopath. "What about Andrea? Is she still alive?"

"I think it's likely. If she wasn't, we would have found her. If he's had other victims, they will have symbolic gravesites. This is a classic escalation pattern. He won't give up until it goes right, which isn't likely. There isn't a woman out there who's going to decide he's Mr. Right after he kidnaps her and shackles and cuffs her prior to proposing. We need to check that whole area for headstones. Check with the gardeners."

"I'm on it." I grabbed another coffee, updated Lieu, and headed out the door. I called the other investigators en route and learned that Andrea's partner had boarded the plane to Aruba. Her boyfriend the PO was turning over rocks in his office and with the probation clients, trying to get a lead. Her parents were aware that she had been stalked but had written it off to the job. The stalking had only gone on for about a week. I made a mental note to ask Kennedy about that.

In the parking lot of the Rose Garden, I had to make several calls to reach the head gardener. She was at home, but getting a home number was like breaking into Fort Knox. She didn't recall running across gravestones or seeing anyone praying in the garden, but a lot of people kneel or squat to get a close look at the flowers. She agreed to be on the lookout and would watch her volunteers for suspicious behavior. I did a brief perusal of the gardens without noticing anything unusual. The gardens covered a large area, and by then it was dark, so I'd have to wait until morning to set up a search team. I called Smitty and stood in front of one of the park signs as I talked to him.

"Hey, boss. Good to see you. Please don't make it obvious, though. He could be watching you."

I stepped away from the sign. "What do you think our next move is?"

"Search the garden first thing in the morning. Process the stone we have for trace evidence or fingerprints. Hope we get lucky."

"Anyone back in the office?" I felt compelled to coordinate the investigation from headquarters.

"Lieu is here. Wants you to get something to eat for us."

I picked up some takeout from Beijing House and headed back to the station. I bought several quarts, and as people filtered in, I gathered what little shreds of evidence we had in exchange for dinner.

Tollie was there to give a final autopsy report on Sanders. "I have never examined a homicide victim with so little trace evidence. I've worked a two-year-old drowning, bodies found in the woods, fire casualties, airplane crash victims, you name it, but never have I come up dry like this. I can tell you how she died—from a lethal injection of drugs. We will have to wait on the toxicology results to know which specific drugs. I can pinpoint approximate time of death, but…"

"What?" I asked, on the edge of my chair.

"I'm afraid I'm not going to be able to save the day. The person responsible for Sanders' death is not your average killer. He had a plan and didn't miss a beat on the clean up. I sent the toxicology samples down to St. Paul and asked them to run secondary tests. I'm hoping additional blood and serum work will tell us more."

"What could we have done differently?"

"Nothing. Everything was bagged, tagged, and collected the way it should have been. Nothing was disturbed, tainted, or destroyed. Everything that should have been done was done. We're just going to have to hope something comes up in the secondaries."

"Larsen has never come up with nothing. I mean never. There has to be something. What did we miss?"

"From what I can see, everything was right from the ID guys. St. Paul will find whatever was missed, if anything was."

I slumped back in my chair. Tollie had never let me down. With the reputation of a bulldog, she's known as a digger to the core. I'd never seen her defeated. I've also never seen her satisfied. She always finds some nit-picking bullshit on how we could have done things better or differently. It's in a medical examiner's nature. Tollie's job was to tell me how someone had died. In this case, I needed more than that. I needed information that would help me keep someone alive.

"I assume you put a rush on the results from St. Paul?"

She looked at me over her glasses. "Yes, I did."

Intruder

Chapter 12

I radioed the remainder of the D's in the field to come in for a briefing at 9 p.m. It had been a long day for everyone. I'm sure many of them had been running movie clip memories of Andrea in the back of their minds all day, just like I had been. I pushed mine down enough to deliver a motivational speech about finding her and holding her captor accountable. I reminded the officers of her tenacity and strength and encouraged them to visualize her alive and fighting. Dismissing them, I told them to get some rest for the next day.

Kennedy and I stayed for shift change. We prepared a briefing with the few details we knew. The night shift, including a small number of neighboring police officers and volunteers, would continue to closely monitor the Rose Garden. A male and female officer were pulled out of uniform to work undercover as homeless people seeking a place to sleep in the park. We even devised a plan to roust them a couple of times during the night, only to have them set up in another location.

I dove into bed with Georgia around midnight. She woke up when I joined her.

"You okay, hon?"

"Beat in all ways. I was this close to him. I'm sure of it."

"This is a hell of a first case for you to jump into as the lead investigator."

"Hell of a case in a lot of ways," I said as I spooned close to her.

"She's a fighter," she said.

"Let's hope."

I'm not sure if I fell asleep at all that night. We both got up at five o'clock. I grabbed a brew and headed to the basement treadmill for a twenty-minute run. She ate cereal in silence on the family room couch to keep me company.

After my workout, I tried to call Alex. He didn't pick up. I sent him a text telling him I loved him and apologizing for being short on his call. I knew Alex, like every teen, was attached at the hip to his phone. He saw it but chose not to respond. I grabbed a handful of protein bars to fuel my day before heading back into the office for the 6:45 a.m. shift change.

The overnight team was all jacked up when I walked in, but it was more from having a driven focus than from unearthing any leads. The town had been eerily quiet with what had been reported as a serial killer on the loose. Smitty, with Corey in tow, briefed me on our surveillance efforts.

These cops had all night to toss ideas around and come up with theories. I wanted to explore their thoughts after I provided some facts. We are trained to be independent thinkers, but this group of cops had been on comparatively boring assignments. I've learned that you need to keep cops informed, or they'll do one of two things, or both. First, they'll freelance. Someone will start thinking about something that should have been done, and rather than ask, they'll do it themselves. This can have disastrous results and has botched more than one case over the years. Second, they'll fill in the blanks. Something that starts as a hypothesis will be fact by the end of the hour. It's usually about the boss or the other shift or something about how the city's going to screw us next. In investigations, it's about how somebody did or didn't do this or that. The golden rule in law enforcement culture is: If you don't hear a rumor by noon, start one. I set out to balance picking their brains with sorting out the facts from the bullshit.

I was relieved that no tragic weddings had been performed in the Rose Garden the previous night, but thinking about what Andrea might be going through made me shudder. She's a fighter, but this perp was a monster. Smitty, Corey, the team, and I spent the next two hours poring over everything we knew and retracing everything we'd done.

The feeling I had was like I was playing a hot game of chess. It's my turn, I've made my move, and my hand's still touching the chess piece. I have the feeling that I've missed something, probably obvious. I'm not looking at my opponent, but I sense he already has his next move planned, and I've set him up for it perfectly. I look at the board and pieces from every angle. I try to think ahead two or three moves. I even squint to try to expose the obscure. Now add an audience, a timer, and the fact that a person's life is at stake. Not just any person—it's Andrea. I pull my hand back from the chess piece, trying to maintain my composure, and hope I'm not missing something.

My cell rings with Georgia's tone, and I flip it open. "What's up?"

"Someone's been in our place! Our house. Someone's been here. I'm scared!" I could hear a shaking in her voice that hadn't ever been there before. She raced through her words.

"Okay, hon. Slow down."

"I came home for an early lunch, and it just felt weird. Normally I can ignore that little voice but this time I know for sure that someone has been in here."

"Get out of there!" I cupped the phone and told Smitty to send cruisers to my house right away.

"She okay, boss?" He stood up.

"Just get some cruisers to my address!" I grabbed my jacket and started running for the parking garage. "Georgia, listen to me. Get out of there now. Go to Buck and Jenny's A squad will be there in two minutes, and I'm on my way."

"Tell me this is not happening to us."

"Get out now! Stay on the phone with me and run over to Buck's."

I could hear Georgia heading down the stairs and out the front door.

"Shit, shit, shit."

"What? Are you okay, babe?"

"I'm so scared. That son of a bitch knows where we live, and he was in our house."

"Georgia. We don't know who it was. This could be some random punk looking for drugs in our medicine cabinet." I tried to calm her and convince myself at the same time. A futile effort in both cases.

"I don't think Jenny's home. Please. Please be home." The door opened, Georgia said something, and the phone went muffled. After a few long seconds, I could hear Georgia's crying voice: "Some son of a bitch was in our home." In the background, I could hear Jenny talking and the sweet sound of sirens. I disconnected.

I radioed the squads, "Just set up a perimeter. Do not make entry or clear the house." If this was my groom and grabber, I didn't want the uniform guys doing a stomp drill on my evidence. "Once you have a solid perimeter, respond to the neighbor's house to the west. The reporting party's there, and she's pretty shook up."

She wasn't the only one who was shook up. I had my car pushed to the limit, and I wasn't catching up to anyone. All the cops were responding like they were headed to their brother's house. In fact, they were. I heard the responding east sergeant report that he was code four with 93's X2. Ninety-three was my radio name, and X2 was a code we all used for our better half. The sergeant was with Georgia at Buck and Jenny's, and all were safe and secure. The hidden message in that code involved the incredibly high rate of divorce in police work. Most of the current spouses were likely an "X" to be.

"What's the plan, boss?" Smitty had been silent the entire trip. I hadn't even realized he was in the car. Corey Groves was in the backseat behind the cage. I was glad to see that he was taking his role in shadowing Smitty seriously.

"I'll need to be with Georgia. You should direct the troops at the house. Let's make sure nobody is still in there, but then slow this whole thing way down. We need to minimize the trample effect."

"I'm on it. You got any pets in there? I'm thinking about sending in a canine to clear the house, keep the traffic down, and limit the trace evidence going in and coming out."

"No pets. Great plan, Smitty."

The neighborhood looked like ground zero. Squads had come out of the woodwork. City, county, troopers—even Mickey the game warden was on site—and they had congregated in large numbers. I was glad we had a plan. Smitty had a canine officer clear the house with a cover officer going in for backup.

Two cops and a dog would preserve the scene nicely. Every cop wanted to go inside, but everyone who goes into a crime scene brings something in with them. The other fact is, everyone who leaves brings something out with them. We needed a break in this case, and the way it was going, our break would likely be subtle. After the micro team cleared the house, Smitty sealed it and called in the crime scene investigators from the lab. I found Georgia in a puddle in Jenny's kitchen. She ran to me, and we held each other for several minutes.

"I'm so scared, Kevin."

"I know. I'm here." We retreated to Buck and Jenny's family room, and I asked the sergeant to keep everyone out for a few minutes. "What happened, sweetie?"

She spoke between sniffling, "I came home to grab an early lunch, keyed my way in, and dropped my purse on the island like I always do. I thought it was weird when I saw the junk drawer open in the kitchen, knowing what a freak you are about never leaving things ajar. I closed the drawer and walked down the hallway toward our bedroom." She paused briefly and leaned into me.

"The pantry door was open, too, and the light was on. The hair on my neck stood up, and that's when I went to the alarm panel in the hallway and pushed the red panic button. The sirens didn't sound, and the button didn't even chime, so I pushed it again. Nothing happened. I ran to the kitchen, pulled my cell from my purse, and called you." She began to cry harder. "The son of a bitch was in our house!"

"We're on it, babe. Probably just some punk, but we are on it. The main thing is you're okay. I don't give a shit about the house. It's you I care about."

I asked Jenny to sit with Georgia and met Buck in the driveway. He had come home from work.

"What the hell, Kevin?"

"Georgia apparently interrupted a burglar, but she's okay."

"In the middle of the day? This isn't connected to that serial killer, is it? Could this be connected?"

"I doubt it. This isn't his M.O. I think this was some punk. Probably looking for cash for dope. Jenny's in there with Georgia. I'll get back to you after I see what the boys have learned so far." The last thing I needed was to have the neighborhood convinced a killer was focusing on our quiet neighborhood. My gut told me he was.

Once our team swept the house, I connected with Smitty. I wanted to make sure they had swept the place for bugs and other electronics. I wasn't about to take any chances with my humble abode.

In the world of law enforcement, we have three zones. In the red zone, we're called to action—adrenaline pumping, life or death, jump into it with everything on full alert. In the yellow zone, we watch… everything… and everyone. If there isn't an arrest or chase going on, we're all in yellow zone all the time unless we're home. Home is the safe zone. Turn it all off, crack a beer, be vulnerable with your wife and kids zone. Chances are, I wouldn't see this space as a green zone for a long, long time now.

"Smitty, over here."

"Hey, boss. How you doing?" he said with a nod.

"Peachy." I gave him a phony smile. "Have you swept it for bugs and electronics?"

"Sorry, don't have the equipment. We don't carry it in our shop, and it's quite expensive."

"Get Larsen in here and see what he can turn up." Smitty radioed the perimeter to send him in.

He was there in a flash, turning the scene into his playground. At first he stood there taking it all in. "You guys pull the alarm panel?" he asked.

I looked at him in dismay and urged him to move in with a rolling motion of my hands. "Look for cameras or a listening device. Do some serious digging. This no-trace crap isn't helping."

"Striker, take a break." Smitty pushed me outside and back to Georgia. I needed to get a grip or risk being pulled from the case.

I hugged Georgia. "Call in Kennedy." I said to Smitty.

He nodded, turned his back, and made the call.

Kennedy arrived at the scene within a half hour. Larsen had turned up nothing yet. She advised us that a tech team would be joining us posthaste. She, Smitty, Corey, Georgia, and I did a walk-through together. According to Kennedy, Georgia's training as a therapist was invaluable in that it might provide us with insights into the intruder's psyche.

Kennedy held us at the door and asked Georgia to go through everything just as she did when she arrived home.

"I came in, put my purse on the island, and right away sensed something was off."

"What sense was awakened? Show us exactly where you were standing," Kennedy directed her. "Good. Now close your eyes. What exactly was the sense?"

"Like a person was here. It smelled off." Georgia opened her eyes and looked down the hall.

"Okay, show us what you did next," Kennedy encouraged her.

"I walked over here toward the pantry, when I noticed the junk drawer open. It looked rifled through. The pantry light was on. I reached in to check the light, but it was switched to detect motion, which told me that someone had passed through recently. When I went into the bedroom, I saw the step stool at the foot of the bed, tipped over. Neither one of us would have done that. I definitely knew someone had been here then."

"Did you hear anything? Think back to when you first came home."

"When I first drove up, I sensed something. Maybe a door slamming. I came in the back and entered into the kitchen." She led us to the front door. It was unlocked.

Kennedy turned to Smitty. "Find out if anyone logged whether this door was locked or unlocked during the sweep."

Smitty ran out the back door with Groves close behind.

Kennedy led us to the bedroom and looked up at the ceiling above the bed. "We'll sweep this whole house, but my money's on the ceiling fan. We need Smitty to take a look at this. What would he be doing with a ceiling fan? I'm also guessing he heard your car and bolted. There's no way he would have left things in this much disarray otherwise." She brightened and almost seemed pleased by the break-in. "I'm hoping he finished the installation before he was interrupted. It would be our first significant lead yet."

"You think this is related to our killer?" I asked.

"My gut says yes, but let's see what the tech team turns up. I want to know how he disabled the alarm. That's not easy."

I looked at Georgia, who had paled considerably. I took her hand and said, "Hon, let's just wait and see. Take one thing at a time." I took her out to sit on the patio with me while we let the sweeper team work with Smitty and Core yin the house. We sat in silence, thinking through all of the possibilities and implications.

In a few minutes, Smitty came out with a big grin on his face. "Look at this friggin' thing Larsen found." He held a tiny ocular device in the palm of his hand.

"Camera?" Georgia asked before I could.

Smitty's exuberance over his find subsided substantially as the impact of what he had discovered was written all over Georgia's face.

"And it was pointed at our bed?"

Smitty nodded.

She looked at me. "You think this is related to your killer?" She seemed angry.

"I do. I'm sorry, hon. I brought a monster into our home." As soon as I said it, she softened.

"You didn't cause this. The monster found us. You try to save people from these bad guys. I just didn't expect one to turn up this close to home. First Andrea, now this. Do you think this is about you? I feel like he's circling us."

I pulled her close. She said what I had been thinking. *What if this sick bastard was circling me, and she was next on his list?* I felt anger, helplessness, and ten other emotions I couldn't pin down. I didn't have words. I stroked her hair and tried to channel those emotions into devising a plan.

Smitty had exited discreetly and gone back into the house. We sat back down on the patio furniture. "Okay, I'm worried, too. But we need to find a way to live that isn't all about fear."

"We can't control our emotions that easily, Kevin," she said in a resigned tone.

"True. I can get you an armed guard, though."

"Besides you?"

"Besides me."

"That will help, but posting a guard won't be conducive to practicing therapy."

"I suppose not. We can check out your waiting area. Find a way to cover the entrance. The guard can be a receptionist in training unless you want to take some time off."

"And what? Sit around being scared? Not going to happen."

"Well, it's a plan anyway." She nodded silently. We walked back into our fingerprint-dust covered house and crime scene. Once all of the techs had cleared out, I got a briefing from Kennedy and Smitty. Long and short of it was, they only found one camera. It was dialed into our wireless router. They were working on figuring out where the signal was transmitting to, but they were less than hopeful. Kennedy felt certain that the killer was fixated on me. She had a sinking feeling that Andrea was no longer with us.

For the rest of the day, I worked from home while trying to reclaim our house. An assigned unit was parked out front, with another unmarked covering the back of the property.

Under Our Noses

Chapter 13

As we finished the cleanup just after 9:00 P.M., I got a call from Smitty. Andrea had been found—alive, but barely hanging on. She'd been left for dead in her unmarked squad on the boulevard in front of the Rose Garden. She'd been posed in the car, but had somehow crawled out and onto the sidewalk, where a jogger found her and called it in. She was in the ICU at St. Francis's in a medically induced coma.

Andrea was still unconscious when Georgia and I arrived at the hospital. She was bruised head to toe with ligature marks on her wrists and ankles. The ambulance crew had bagged up her belongings, including the wedding dress in which she was found. The doctor said she was drugged enough to kill a horse, but something must have been haywire about how she metabolized the meds. It was difficult to estimate how long she would need to be unconscious.

I struggled to maintain my composure as we stood at the bedside. Andrea and I had been intimate. Passionate in our lovemaking and fights in equal measure. She was close to unrecognizable beneath her now-discolored bruises. Georgia put her arm around me.

"She lived through it. That's something."

" I know, but it's a lot to take in. I usually don't know the victims. I wasn't prepared for this."

"Do you have to remain lead investigator?" she asked.

"Not sure. It could provide the defense a reason to attack our evidence. On the other hand, everyone knows Andrea. She's one of us."

"Not everyone slept with her."

Her comment struck me as harsh. She could have chosen other words to say the same thing. I guessed she was having feelings of jealousy or insecurity or both. I remained silent, but I'm sure she felt me stiffen.

"I think I'll have Kennedy run point on Andrea's statement." I stepped outside the room to make the call. Kennedy was parking in the hospital ramp when I reached her. We talked briefly, and she agreed to handle all matters relating directly to Andrea. I would help her navigate our techies and lab as well as keep her connected to the rest of the bureaucracy.

Georgia and I went to the coffee shop and sipped without talking as hospital staff and family members of the patients filtered in and out. At some point I emerged from my solemn grieving to realize that Georgia's silence likely had to do with how utterly upside down our sweet home life had become. I looked into her eyes to search for answers, paralyzed by the idea that we were having ex issues between us.

"You okay?" I ventured tentatively.

"No. Not even close."

"What do you need?"

"A new house, and for Andrea to be all right."

"Are you serious on the house?"

"Maybe."

"We can go to a hotel," I offered, shrugging off my own need for the comforts of home.

"I think that would be good. At least for tonight. I'm shot. I need sleep."

"I'll have Kennedy call me with any updates."

She gave me a look that said *Pull your head out of your ass, you idiot. Too much has happened to us for you to be telling me about work. Just be here for me.* I felt shame at my insensitivity. Why on earth was she with a clod like me?

We stayed at the Radisson. It was two blocks from the Police Department, and Georgia could walk the six blocks to her office, but I drove her to work the next morning after a squad delivered a change of clothes from our house. We didn't talk much before bed, or in the morning. We agreed to text each other periodically throughout the day, and I paid for another night's stay at the Radisson. Her first text arrived just as I sat down at my desk with a fresh cup of coffee.

"It's good to be at work. I feel a little saner here. I'm sorry I was so harsh with you. I love you and the work you do."

"Thanks, hon. I'm sorry about all of this. I love you, too."

"I'm going to spar with Heather at the karate studio after work. I'll have the guard drop me at the hotel." She signed off with a smiley face, and I felt relieved. If anything could help her get past the invasion of our home, it would be her karate.

Smitty and Corey walked in looking disheveled. "This data tracking is giving us fits. He has the signal bouncing all over the place, including in and out of two other countries. If there is a way to find the final destination, I'll find it. We'll find it." He elbowed Corey. "This kid is good. Where did you find him?"

"I got lucky," I admitted.

"Get any sleep?" he inquired, showing uncharacteristic empathy.

"Couple of hours. You?"

"Five." He plowed back into his work. It's no wonder I have no life partner skills. This is how cop partners support each other. We are brief and curt. The case takes precedence.

She Remembers a Wedding

Chapter 14

Kennedy came in around nine and requested a briefing in the small conference room she had claimed as her office. Kennedy, I noticed, did have people skills. She missed nothing. I suppose she was trained to pick up on moods and nonverbals. Profilers are part psychologist, part cop—maybe similar to a combination of Georgia and me. I'd bolster up the courage to ask her how she made all of that fit together once this whole thing was done.

She asked me how I was doing before we dug into the briefing. No pure cop would do that. The only time we asked that question was when we were certain an officer was fine, and we were trying to get the other cop to see it.

"I'll live," I said, irritated at how vulnerable I felt.

She took my cue and moved into the briefing.

"She was raped and cleaned up just like Sanders was. It looks to me like these are patterned crimes. He's working out some deep-seated grief, loss, or rejection. He's a serial killer, and he's not going to stop until he completely decompensates or we catch him. I'm pretty sure he already has another victim."

"Crap," I muttered.

"I stayed with Andrea last night. She's awake, but her stream of consciousness is severely compromised. She remembers a wedding, but she thinks she married you."

I blinked. I tried to take in what she was saying. I blinked again. "Me? What do you make of that?"

"I can't make that leap yet." She raised her shoulders a tad. "Either you are in her subconscious as someone she would like to wed, or something happened with him that led her to believe she was with you." She seemed to be watching me for a reaction.

"She may have seen him kill Genevieve. Her words aren't cohesive yet, or her thoughts. I can tell she's struggling to sort memory from drug-induced perception. She kept mentioning Minnesota. She said it several times. I don't know what it means yet. There is an association there, and it's strong, but she isn't thinking clearly."

"Can she ID him?" I asked.

"She thinks she was with you." I felt her eagle eyes on me again. It dawned on me that she was trying to gage whether or not I could have played a part in this.

"Holy shit," I said. "Good thing I had the sense to call you in on this."

"Yes. Good thing indeed. For her and for you."

"Do we know when she was placed in the car? Was she there while we did our search of the area?"

"It looks that way, but we may never know for sure."

"Damn. She was right there. I was probably within a block of where her car was. Did that hurt her medically? How could we have missed that?"

"They can't say when she was placed in the car or how long she remained there. They aren't sure why her metabolism is off, either. It definitely saved her life."

"Could her car have been moved there after we searched? Or was it found where she originally parked?"

"She radioed in her time of arrival when she joined the surveillance team working in the vicinity of the Rose Garden."

"So he would've had to see her exit that car in order to place her back in it," I guessed.

"Or he could have tried the keys to an obvious unmarked car. Or he knew her."

"What do you think the significance of placing her in the car was?"

"Well, it could be a message to us that he can operate right under our noses. 'See how smart I am. You can't catch me.' But that is speculation. We can be sure of one thing, though. He is watching…" She circled her index finger in the air and then pointed it at me. "And I believe this revolves around you somehow. I don't know how or why yet. It could be from a past association or just that you were lead on investigating his first kill. Do you have any theories?"

I struggled to see any ties. I wasn't ready to voice my concerns about Smitty. If he was involved, I trusted Kennedy's instincts and training a hell of a lot better than my own at that point. Unless I was one hundred percent sure, I wasn't going to drag his name through the mud. Cops don't do that to other cops, and especially not to their partners.

She saw the wheels turning in my head and waited. It unnerved me. "Are you sure you don't have more of a tie to Genevieve Sanders?" she asked.

"I didn't sleep with her if that's what you're implying," I said defensively.

"Any relationship?" she continued. "She interviewed me once." I gave her the rundown. She brightened at the mention of footage and asked where she could get the tape for a look.

Back Home
Chapter 15

Things seemed to have ground to a halt in the investigation. Smitty and his sidekick had made zero progress tracking the electronic transmission to a source. Kennedy had returned to the hospital but didn't learn anything new from Andrea. Andrea was waking up sporadically, but still confused about her memories. The toxicology results had come back, and the drugs in her system were a combination of a date rape drug and a tranquilizer. Because Andrea's squad had been found near the Rose Garden, we concentrated our efforts there. Officers were assigned to canvass that neighborhood. Isolating significant leads in such a public and busy place would be difficult, however.

I was restless, anxious, and feeling the pressure. The chief and the mayor had both called to inquire about progress in the case. I got the distinct feeling that if we didn't get on top of this case soon, another cop would head my unit in the future. The press hounded us, so I put an email warning out to the department to direct all press inquiries to me or to the chief. I knew if I didn't show some progress, the chief would throw me under the bus. This was the first known serial killer in Duluth. Or rather, attempted serial killer. I had to believe Andrea was going to make it. Thankfully, the press hadn't used that terminology…yet. We had to find a new avenue to pursue. I paced around the interior confines of the first floor of the station and suddenly got an idea. I strongly believed the perp was focusing on me, and that might help us. I had to do something. If not for me, for Georgia. It was a simple idea, really.

We could bait the perp. The public had all but stopped using the Lakewalk. I'd fill it with attractive female cops and dress them to look like Georgia. The bait would walk, run, and do whatever they could to resemble Georgia. Each female officer on the force who remotely looked like Georgia would take at least one walk or run per shift in undercover clothing. Even the female officers in higher administrative positions stepped up. I scheduled slots on a sign-in board, and Smitty and Corey set up a station to outfit them with a wire so he could monitor them audibly while maintaining surveillance via the previously installed cameras. It wasn't much, but we had a plan.

Georgia had sent me a couple of "*Hey, thinking of you*" texts throughout the day, and she walked to the station after her sparring match with an unmarked squad following her by half a block.

We mutually agreed to give home a try. We were not only sick of the hotel, and missing our home, but neither one of us wanted to have our lives ruled by fear. Before I left, I stuck my nose in Kennedy's office. "Need anything?"

"Not right now. How was the Radisson?"

"Okay. It's close, clean, decent restaurant, but I hate it. It's not home. Where have you been staying?"

"Hotel 6 by the mall. I'd like to get closer."

"We've decided to go back home. Why don't you come and stay with us. We have a basement room with a private bath."

She pondered that. Was she thinking she could get closer to a person of interest in the case? Maybe she hated hotels.

"Sounds great. You sure I won't be imposing?"

"Not at all. One more trained cop with a gun in the house would be welcome right now."

I gave her the address and shared the news with Georgia on the way home. She seemed to like the idea. I think she looked forward to having a psychologist to talk to in light of the recent break-in.

We stopped at a grocery store on the way home, and I could tell Georgia was thrilled at the idea of cooking for our guest. She picked up ingredients for antipasto and grilled tilapia. While we shopped, she filled me in on her sparring match. She had a fresh bruise on her cheek but glowed with excitement.

"Heather is really good. I'm learning things from her. She fights hard, and she says she's impressed with my kicks."

"I'm doubly impressed," I said as we rolled into the driveway. She got busy in the kitchen caramelizing onions and creating a red sauce to drizzle over the fish. She made a side of golden braised artichokes with garlic and mint. The pots clanked loudly as she sang a tune from her childhood. If I could just keep her cooking, we might get through this. I didn't care how many pots were stacking up in the sink for me to wash.

I put on some light jazz and helped Georgia, chopping onions and garlic and stirring this or that. Kennedy walked in to a house full of delicious smells, and a decent home feeling.

I showed her to her basement suite, and she joined us after a quick shower. Over dinner, the two women talked about their various studies in psychology, and I knew it had been a good move inviting Kennedy to stay with us. They went out to the patio while I happily cleaned up the dishes.

Home Invasion

Chapter 16

We all settled in the basement family room after I finished the dishes. Kennedy opted for a soda, while Georgia and I had a beer. I suspected Kennedy wanted to stay sharp. There were clearly some things I could learn from her. We worked our way through conversations about politics, religion, and cop mentality. Things I would avoid talking about with most people. The two of them seemed to like to be able to deconstruct cops without losing sight of that altruistic drive fueling the good ones. We all started to fade just short of talking about bad cops. Before we turned in, Kennedy spoke to me in private while we did a perimeter check on the property.

"I pulled the tape of the interview you did with Genevieve Sanders. It was interesting." She had my attention.

"Interesting how?" I asked.

"Well, it wasn't the interview per say but her feelings for you." I raised my head in surprise.

"As the program started, she straightened your collar. It was subtle, but clearly affectionate. She appeared to be quite smitten with you. Did she ask you out?"

"Wow. Not that I recall."

"I also watched the interaction after you went off air. Her body language spoke volumes. She had a thing for you." I shook my head in disbelief.

"I remember thinking that she was a good interviewer. She got right to the heart of the matter. She was really upset that the director of a nonprofit helping the poor would steal from his own organization and from the people the organization was supposed to be helping, but I didn't remember feeling or noticing an attraction."

"Well, Striker, you're not so tuned into a lot of things." She smiled, obviously amused. "I'm thinking that if this guy is focused on you and had access to these tapes, we just found a tie to you for both victims."

We did the perimeter check together and checked in with the two squads. There was a weakness in the surveillance of the backyard where the north neighbor's fence joined ours. Before turning in, I asked the alley squad to do a walk by periodically. I lay awake for hours, listening to the creaks of our house and the tick-tock of a clock in the kitchen. I had never realized how loud the hum of our refrigerator was before that night. At around two o'clock, I finally gave up on sleeping and wandered out to the kitchen to rummage around in the fridge. I had an armful of food when suddenly I felt the butt of a gun jammed into my right temple. I instinctively pulled to the side and spun around, knocking something off of the counter. The next thing I knew, I was on the ground with a forearm to my throat. It was dark, but

I could tell my assailant had a ski mask on. He held the gun to my head and whispered, "Shut the fuck up if you want to live even a minute more." His eyes were dark. The pupils of his eyes were so big I couldn't distinguish the color. I reared up and cut his legs out with my legs while twisting. The gun went off with a deafening blast right before everything went black.

I came to on the living room floor with my feet elevated and an EMT holding smelling salts under my nose. Georgia and Kennedy hovered above me.

"Was I shot?"

"Knocked out." Kennedy said.

"With the gun?"

She nodded yes.

"What else happened?"

Kennedy volunteered her version. "As I came up the stairs, I saw Georgia kick the living shit out of the guy. I mean literally. I don't know how he walked out of here." She looked at Georgia with respect. "She kicked the gun out of his hand after he hit you with it. Then she kicked him in the head, the chest, and pretty much out the door. She knocked the screen door right off of the hinges. Somehow he got past the two squads. We haven't figured out how yet."

Georgia kneeled beside me. "You saved my life," I said with some amazement.

"I wish I hadn't kicked him out that door. I'd still be kicking," Georgia said in an angry tone.

"Unreal," was all I could manage.

"I concur," said Kennedy.

I had to be cleared at the hospital before we all returned home. Kennedy drove us and paid a visit to Andrea while they gave me a battery of tests. I was sent home with a cautionary "take it easy" warning. Georgia was told to watch me for a change in personality or awareness. I had a splitting headache.

On the way home, Kennedy said that Andrea kept repeating "Minnesota, Minnesota." She had taken a turn for the worse, slipping in and out of consciousness during the last few hours. They were concerned that the drugs she had been given were stored in her liver and continued to be released in small amounts. They had discovered a liver problem that they were struggling to treat. I was too tired to think about going somewhere else for the night, and Kennedy assured me that stepping up the surveillance would keep us safe. I found out in the morning that she slept sitting in a chair right outside our bedroom door.

When I got up, Kennedy had some questions for me. Georgia made us breakfast, and we settled outside on the patio with coffee.

"So, did he say anything to you?"

"Shut the fuck up if you want to live even a minute more."

"You're clear on that. Those were his exact words?"

"That's what I remember. He whispered it."

"Interesting. Either he knew I was in the house, or he didn't want to wake Georgia."

"Why didn't he kill me?"

"He wanted to play with you first. He would have. This guy gets off on power."

"Why didn't he want to wake Georgia?"

"Well, either you were the target and he wanted to take his time, or she was and he still didn't want to miss an opportunity to kill you slowly. He could also have just been getting his bearings. Being careful. My take is this guy is organized and smart. He is a long way from decompensating. If we don't catch him, he will kill again. Soon."

I didn't want to hear that. "Why did you wait until today to talk to me?" It didn't seem like good police work to me.

"You had a concussion. I couldn't trust your memories. Today might have been a crapshoot, too, but you seem pretty clear-headed. Do you remember anything else?"

"His eyes." She nodded, wanting me to elaborate. "His pupils were huge. I couldn't even tell what color his eyes were. It was dark, but that struck me."

"Hmm. It was dark, and he might have been high on adrenalin. That could be all of it, or he could be on drugs. I'll have to consult with someone about chemicals that make the pupils dilate. Chemicals make sense, though. He's using them to drug his victims. It might even be a steroid." She went inward for a minute, working on the problem. "Do you remember anything else?"

"I do," Georgia piped up "His smell."

Kennedy nodded. "Can you describe it?"

"Musky. Strong. Male."

"Nothing store-bought?"

"No."

"Height?" She looked at both of us.

"Six-two?"

Georgia nodded agreement. "That's my take, too."

"Strong in a wiry sort of way," I said. "He had me pinned quickly—like he's had training and experience. I'm strong and big and could muscle him off once I got my bearings, but he knew how to use moves and the element of surprise."

"So he likely works out at a gym, or has extensive tactics training." Kennedy mused

Closer to Home

Chapter 17

Wednesday was cloudy and cool. The weather channel predicted that the clouds would burn off around noon. I went into work, and so did Georgia. I felt the PD was the safest place for me, even with my headache. Georgia was confident she could take care of herself, given her actions the night before. Everything looked like it was on track until I didn't get the first text. I knew her patients were hourly, and she may have forgotten to send the first one, but I wasn't taking any chances. I called her office. Her coworker picked up.

"Mr. Dexter, I'm glad you called. Is Georgia all right?"

My heart pounded in my chest. "What do you mean?"

"Is she coming in?"

"She's not there?" *Stupid question.* "You haven't seen her at all?"

"No."

"Have you been there all morning?"

"Yes. Why?"

"A squad dropped her there this morning. Could you please call me immediately if she shows up?"

"Of course."

I hung up without saying thank you and called Officer Mike Waldo, who had dropped her off. "Did you see her go into the building?"

"Yes." He sounded scared.

"Did you walk her up to her office?"

"No. Should I have?"

"She's not there, damn it! Go back and question bystanders. I'm on my way."

I quickly called Kennedy and updated her as I ran to my squad. I sped to Georgia's office with my siren screaming in perfect harmony with my headache. Waldo pulled up when I did. We both tried to walk up to the building rather than run. He was afraid for his job, and I was afraid for Georgia's life. The only thing that kept me from taking it out on him was my desperate need to find her.

I took the stairs two at a time and pointed him toward the elevator. Trying to calm myself, I pushed open the door to the waiting area. I asked the receptionist to join me in Georgia's office. I didn't want to upset the clients. When Mike came in, he stood quietly outside the door awaiting my instructions.

"Please check out back." I pointed to my eyes with two fingers. I hoped he would understand that to mean, "Look for signs of a struggle." Connie sat down in one of the therapy chairs. "What's happening?"

"I don't know. Georgia didn't show up here this morning?"

"No."

"What time did you get here?" I was trying to speak in a

normal tone of voice. My head was pounding, and visions of Georgia kidnapped by that monster were creeping uninvited into my imagination.

"Seven."

"And Georgia usually arrives at seven-thirty, right?"

"Right."

"Was her office open when you got here?"

"No."

"And when she didn't come in at seven-thirty, why didn't you call me?" I knew this was irrational.

"I called the house. What's going on?"

"I'm sorry. It's not your fault. Call me if she shows up, please." I handed her my card and went outside to find Mike. He had just done a perimeter check around the back of the building and was headed toward me. He held out his hand.

"Are these her keys?"

I didn't have gloves on. I resisted the urge to touch them. "Yes. That's her gym pass." I could see the door fob with the karate logo and her distinctive monogrammed key chain. I had glanced at them a hundred times on our kitchen island. *Damn. Damn. Damn. Her monogrammed key chain.*

"What time did you drop her off?"

"Seven twenty-five."

I wanted to punch him square in the face. He had done the same thing yesterday, and nothing had happened. This wasn't yesterday. This was the day after she had kicked the shit out of the kidnapper. She had won. He had lost face, and now she was going to pay. I was going to pay. I told Waldo to continue canvassing the block to see if anyone had seen anything. Then I raced back to the station to consult with Kennedy. She had to profile this. We had to find Georgia – now.

I don't remember driving to the station, but somehow I ended up there, and somehow I ended up pacing in Kennedy's make-do office racing through an explanation about how Georgia ended up missing. The profiler spoke to me in soothing tones, and when that didn't help, got sharp with me.

"Striker, knock it off. Tap into your training. Turn your reptilian brain off. She needs you right now."

That got my attention. Someone shoved a cup of coffee in front of me with a bottle of ibuprofen. My head pounded, so I swallowed four pills and took several deliberate deep breaths.

"This is not your fault. Finding fault right now is a waste of time. We need to focus. Clear your mind of the images of what may be happening to her. She's as strong as any woman I know. Physically and psychologically."

That helped. I replaced the images of her being tortured with ones of her planning a way out and kicking the shit out of him again.

"Okay, I can do this. Let's run down what we have so far," I said.

"Let me sum it up," she said with confidence. "He's six foot two; wiry, strong, and trained. He has issues with women, and more likely, with marriage or commitment. He's smart and organized. He has skills in media and a knack for electronics. He has a need to pose his victims either for himself, the police, the public, or all three. He has a fixation with you. We don't know why yet. He dresses his victims in high-end wedding dresses that are quite old. We have to get someone else tracking that down. You and Smitty have too much on your plate to do that justice."

I cut in, "Smitty thought we should go after Dean Jones, the Channel 7 makeup guy who was close to Genevieve. Maybe he was right."

Kennedy frowned. "I don't think he fits the profile, so it likely would be a waste of your time. I would bet my career that our killer is heterosexual. He stalks his prey and makes sure they know he's focusing on them. That's either an escalation in his fantasy, or he's building terror. He has a strong focus on the Rose Garden, in all likelihood due to the wedding/commitment angle. He takes another victim before he dumps the one he has abducted. He may be involving them in this fantasy by forcing them to watch or participate. He uses drugs to subdue his victims and keeps them for days at a time." She stopped, scratched her head, walked a complete circle around the table before stopping at the white board.

"Here is where his first two victims were left." She drew a crude picture of the Rose Garden, placing X's where the victims were found. "The first one had a much higher degree of effort and drama. He took his time staging and posing the scene." She stopped to look at me for emphasis.

"The second victim was staged, but not nearly to that degree. I'm guessing it's because we were watching. He still had to put her in the Rose Garden, even though we were all over it. That's key. We need to focus there." She circled the Rose Garden. "He probably can't break that pattern. The first one was risky because he took so long with the staging. The second was risky because it was right under our noses."

I felt hopeful. We had something.

"Do we put the pressure on? Cover every inch with uniforms, lights and sirens, or go in stealthily?"

"One more thing for the profile." She looked me in the eyes. "He's ex-military or a cop."

My mind went to Smitty. He was the right height, former military, and a cop. My pulse pounded. She saw my reaction. *Damn.*

"What?" she probed.

"It's stupid. There is no way he could have pulled this off and kept doing the job."

"Who?" She leaned in with a deliberate stare, willing me to tell on my partner.

"Smitty."

She nodded. "I agree. Pretty hard to do the job and pull it off. Not impossible, but extremely hard."

She didn't say right off that she didn't think it was him. "What are your concerns about him? What put that seed of doubt in your mind?"

I got up and paced. I started ticking off things with my fingers. "Number one: He 'slept through' the Genevieve Sanders crime scene discovery with a lame excuse. Number two: He could have been at the Rose Garden when I chased the bastard. Number three: Georgia had told me he prowls women. She said it was just a matter of time before he hit on her just because she's my girlfriend. Number four: He has issues. Big issues. He's a ticking time bomb in a nice suit most of the time. PTSD. Whatever. Number five: He's prior military and a cop. Number six: He's skilled in electronics." I watched her for a response.

"So we watch him. Change nothing. He's a person of interest," she said calmly. "That's why Corey is shadowing him, right?"

"Right."

"For the record, that was a good move. Also for the record, you should have voiced your concerns with me."

I felt like a shit for accusing my partner.

The minutes were creeping their way toward noon, and we were getting nowhere. The kidnapper has had five hours with Georgia. A lot could happen in five hours. Screw my loyalty to a partner.

Corey Groves was tagging along with Smitty as ordered. Unfortunately, he also seemed to be bonding with him. When I pulled the younger officer aside to question him about Smitty's whereabouts at 7:30 that morning, he showed a budding loyalty that gave me misgivings.

"He drove himself to work this morning and arrived at 8 a.m. as expected," he said.

"And you don't know where he was prior to that?"

"No, you didn't say I had to bunk with him, too," Corey replied hotly. "We were up late last night as it was."

"And you don't want to think he's a serial killer, do you? Well, neither do I." That got his attention. "If it turned out to be one of us, we'd all be blamed. We'd lose the public trust. And yet Smitty fits the profile. I was hoping you could help us eliminate him as a suspect."

"Oh,... no, I guess I can't help this time," he reddened. "It's your X2 I heard. I'm sorry. It's just hard. Cops are supposed to back each other up."

"You're right," I said. "But more important than that is uncovering the truth, solving the case, you know? We have to be relentless about that. More relentless than the crooks. Do you understand?"

"Yes, sir." Fervor returned to his boyish features. "I'll stay on him."

A Plan

Chapter 18

Somehow I managed to pull it together to regroup for yet another command central. We pulled in every on- or off-duty law enforcement officer from the PD and surrounding areas again. The ones who weren't on the clock came in on their own time. Kennedy and I put a map of the Rose Garden and surrounding one-mile area on the white board in as much detail as we could. We assigned cops to play the role of runners, walkers, roller-bladers, women pushing strollers, and couples. We had a schedule worked out with staggered reporting-in times. Two phone operators relayed information to us. Smitty watched the cameras while I watched him. We set up a couple arguing, a would-be drug deal going down, a street vendor getting rousted for not having the correct permit, as well as a saxophone player performing for tips. The cops who looked like obvious cops played the rousters. We covered the area like a blanket.

Officers canvassed local stores and shops. The perp could easily be an employee at any number of local shops, including a hardware store, auto parts store, fitness center, grocery store, and last but not least, a bridal shop. We knocked and talked our way across the square mile and then some.

I kept a running list of locations on one of the white boards with sticky notes that could be moved around. I updated them as information came in. The day grinded on. It drove me crazy to be heading the investigation from inside, but I knew that once we found even the smallest thread, I would grab onto it and zero in on the suspect. We just needed a break. As night rolled in, we ordered Chinese. My head had pounded all day, but it seemed a welcome distraction. It was just painful enough to keep me from going insane with worry over Georgia. I was tense and could feel my anger building to the point where I wished I had a punching bag.

Just as I thought that, Kennedy approached, looking concerned. "What do you need?"

"A punching bag."

"Not a bad idea, actually. I'll work on it." She left the room. It was weird. After ten minutes, she stepped back in and said, "One's on the way. Did you mean a speed bag or a big bag?" She was dead serious. I stood with my mouth agape.

"I called the local fighting gym. They're donating one for the cause. We have to bring it back when we're done, though. I didn't know which one you wanted, so I borrowed both. Gloves, too." She put her hands on her hips and smiled.

"Thanks."

"You're under a tremendous amount of stress. I think this may keep you from doing anything stupid." She smiled again.

"That obvious, huh?"

She waved her hand. "It's what I do."

When the bags arrived, I pounded the big bag, letting off some steam and picturing the killer's eyes with each punch.

"Anything come back yet on the dilated pupils?" I asked her, still breathing hard.

"I have the team working on it. They're identifying drugs that could do that without rendering him nonfunctional. Right now, the theory is that it was a combination of the light and his adrenaline. Most of the performance-enhancing drugs we know about would constrict his pupils. A lot of minds are researching it, but we have nothing solid yet." She looked at me closely. "Did you come up with anything else when you hit the bag? Anything at all? You're the only one with a clear memory who's been in close contact with him."

"No."

"Go hit it some more. You need to let go. Let your fears and emotions surface. It might give us something."

I went to work on it. The more I hit, the more I needed to go after him. Without a doubt, I would strike first if given the chance. It was me against him. I slammed the bag with my fists. Kennedy came into my field of vision and stood quietly until I stopped. It took me a full minute to catch my breath.

"I need to go after him," I said through ragged breaths.

"Good. Let's do it in a controlled way so that we can watch without being seen. Let's stage a fight between me and you in the Rose Garden. You want to… need to be there, and I tell you to back off. That you'll screw it all up. You go off on me, and I storm off. If he's watching, it will be hard for him to resist coming to you in some way. You'll be in extreme danger."

"What about Georgia? Would this put her in more danger, too?"

"Crapshoot. Could go either way. We're seeing zero progress right now, though, and the clock is ticking." It was dinnertime, and Georgia had been gone since morning. We were well within the critical forty-eight hours, but this case was anything but ordinary.

"Let's do it."

Be Strong

Chapter 19

We staged the fight.

"We have nothing. I need more help from you."

"I've given you plenty, you don't listen."

"I am getting crucified by the chief. The public needs answers." I screamed it in her face.

"Then do your job." She moved into my space a tad more and stormed off.

I paced for a full minute pretending to still be angry and then my cell beeped a text. It was from Georgia's phone. My pulse spiked as I pulled up a picture of her bound, gagged, and drugged. She was sitting in a chair. Her eyes were half shut. I called Kennedy as I scanned the area. I couldn't see anything.

"He just sent me a text picture of her. From her phone."

"Get back here with it. We need Smitty to do his magic—pin the cell tower down and blow the picture up."

"He's watching me right now. I feel it." I looked everywhere. I couldn't see anything or anyone suspicious. I fought the urge to stay put, but I couldn't follow up on this new evidence without Smitty's help. I raced back to the station, dropped my phone on his desk, and hovered as he plugged it into his computer.

"Are you primary on the cell account? Both phones?" Smitty asked.

"Yes."

"Good! Then we don't need a warrant."

"Picture first. We need to identify where she is."

He saved an original untouched version to a jump drive and a network drive, then edited a copy by sharpening the background one area at a time. Corey was set up on a similar computer, running parallel work to see which one of them could come up with a better image. It sickened me to see Georgia held captive, but she was alive. I fought to keep down what little was in my stomach. Smitty worked on the picture a little more before emailing it to the laptop attached to the smart board. After pulling the picture up on the smart board, he adjusted the colors again.

"Okay, it looks to me like this is a warehouse or an old building. See the elongated windows." He used a pointer on the smart board. "This molding here."

Kennedy stepped up to take a closer look. "Yes. We need to get an architectural expert in here. Nail down the year it was built." She looked at me.

"Planning and zoning. It's down the block. I'm on it." I ran through the underground tunnel, swiping my key card to gain access to the off-limits areas, until I reached the planning and zoning offices on the fourth floor of the government services building. I made a pretty spectacular scene as I ran into planning, demanding that their architectural expert accompany me. Once I badged him and explained the situation we were in, he ran back through the tunnel with me.

At the PD, Smitty took me aside as the architectural guy studied the photos. "The cell tower is downtown. He's somewhere below the hill. He could be anywhere east of Messaba Avenue and anywhere south of Skyline Parkway."

"That's a big area," I said with impatience.

"It's more than we had yesterday," he said defensively.

I nodded. "Good point, and good work." I joined the small group of people studying the picture.

"See this door molding?" The zoning guy pointed with his hand instead of using the electronic pointer. "It's circa 1940 to 1947. A local lumber mill produced this molding and sold it to contractors."

"How many buildings are we talking about?" I interjected.

"Right. Well, that's the hard part. There was a big building boom in Duluth during that time period. The lumber and shipping industries were making quite a few millionaires hereabouts. Of course, by then most of the residential mansions of Duluth were built already, but dozens more were constructed during the boom." He sensed my impatience.

"I'm guessing roughly ten warehouses were permitted around then. And some of the houses had large enough floor plans to have tall windows in them like the ones in this picture." He gazed at the projected image.

"Can we get a listing of them?" My patience was wire thin. He knew what we were up against. I didn't give a shit about having a history lesson right then.

"I'm afraid no such list exists. I can have my team go through our records and memory banks and try to come up with a list."

"Please do," I said with some exasperation. "Can you list them in proximity to the Rose Garden? In fact, if you happen across any within close proximity, I want to hear about it right away. We need this done like right now!"

He left in a trot that gave me some satisfaction that he had grasped how critical this information was to our investigation.

"What about her phone?" I asked Smitty.

"Not her phone. It's a clone. He's quite clever."

My head snapped around. "How do you clone a phone?" I asked him.

"Well, you can do it pretty easily if you have the phone in front of you. You'd need the electronic serial number. Then you just reprogram the new phone to have the same phone number. You can transfer everything from the SIM card that way too."

"Why do you think he's doing that?" I asked him.

"I think he's taking the pictures with his phone so that he can keep them, and he programs it as a clone to hers so we can't find him."

"As in trophy pictures?" I wanted that punching bag so bad right then that Smitty stepped away from me.

"We find that phone, and it's better than a confession." He tried to appease me.

"Right." I took some deep breaths. He was being so helpful, but I couldn't forget about the angry, predatory side of him—a side that I'd seen brief flashes of. On the other hand, he was standing right in front of me. He couldn't be torturing Georgia in this moment.

Kennedy took me by the arm and guided me over to a chair in her makeshift office. She poured me a cup of coffee and sat next to me in silence.

I pictured Georgia and reached out to her in my mind. I sent her a mental text. *Hang in, babe. Be strong. I'm coming.*

A Lead or Too Easy?

Chapter 20

We made a plan for Kennedy to check in on Andrea while Smitty dug deeper into the camera signal and cloned phone, and I would drive to the Rose Garden to see what I could get from another visual of the area. The killer had to be close or watching electronically. I knew he was jerking on my chain with Georgia, and it hurt. I was so angry I was unable to focus. I pictured her in our basement recreation room practicing her karate. Then I shook off the memories.

Sitting there on a bench near the wedding arch, I looked around at the nearby buildings, scanning them for a "built in 1940-something" sign. An officer watched me from half a block away. Was he assigned to me in case I drew out the killer or because I was a key suspect? Why had Andrea thought she was marrying me? Why was the killer focused on me? Who on earth did I know besides Smitty who had hang-ups with women? Shit, it could be anyone I ever arrested or even gave a speeding ticket to, for that matter. No, that doesn't make sense, either. He's driven by psychological problems. He's a nut job about marriage and commitment, chasing some fantasy he thinks he can make into reality. I was coming up with zip. Smitty was the only screwed-up guy I knew.

I got up to take a closer look at a nearby building—I could just make out its top floor to the east of the garden. As I approached it, my phone rang. It was Kennedy.

"Where are you?"

"Rose Garden. Just walking down toward the old Armory building. It looks to be about the right age." I was a quarter of a block away.

"Stop," she said

I stopped. "Why?"

"It's our best lead yet. It was built in 1947, and the inscription on the building reads 'For a Strong Minnesota.'"

"She might be in there." My pulse quickened. I wanted to go in gun blazing, find Georgia, and kill the monster. Not necessarily in that order.

"Get back here, and assemble a tactical team. You go in there alone, and you're much more likely to get her killed than to rescue her. He has the advantage. He would probably see you coming. "Don't run! He'll know something's up."

I forced myself to walk slowly to my car, refraining from peeling out of the lot and back to the station. Good police work would include having someone sit on the Armory while the team formed, but I don't want to be the one assigned to sit on it.

By the time I got back to the station, half of the tactical team was in the turnout room putting on their gear. They had the punching bag ready for me, and I went a few rounds, trying to settle my rage and nerves as I listened to the clank of metal and armor readying around the room.

Captain Korda, the head of tactical, projected two images on the smart board. One was the blueprint of the building, and another was a satellite image of the block the old Armory was situated on. We had a personnel count of twenty-two including Kennedy and me. Korda divided the officers up into colored squads—blue, green, and yellow—one color for each entrance. A leader was designated for each team, and was assigned floors. The teams would time their stairwell ascents, as there was only one stairwell. Another squad of seven would protect the perimeter from both inside and outside threats, and would storm the succinct area identified as the hostage target. We would go in as fast as possible. Korda was waiting for delivery of the search warrant as he briefed the group. Each team had a pair of entry guys armed with MP-5 submachine guns, a gas guy who had flash bangs and an array of gas delivery armaments, two shot gunners (one with slugs and one with military buckshot for close encounters), and a tail gunner to cover our rears.

These were weapons that were meant for fighting. The handguns we carried each day were incredibly inadequate for the job. Stopping someone with a handgun requires a shot directly to the head or a vital organ. Even then, it can take multiple shots and time. The handguns we carried were best used to fight our way to the long guns we all have in our cars, and every officer knows that. The long guns have stopping power, mostly because of the speed of their projectiles.

"We'll have two snipers positioned on two adjoining buildings with a view into the top floor of the Armory. They should be just about set, and I expect an initial report anytime."

The warrant arrived, and Korda read it aloud to the group. It allowed entry into the property with the sole purpose of locating hostage Georgia Frank and/or any other hostage unknown at the present time. Any evidence in support of murder or hostage taking could be confiscated for further investigation and evidence at trial.

Korda asked in his former Marine voice: "Good to go?" The groups hustled out of the briefing room.

We parked the tactical van between the front and rear doors of the Armory, and several other vehicles parked at perimeter locations. The teams sat silent and still as Korda recited the plan from memory. We were to communicate via our tactical radios. The building had six floors with east and west corridors. "Four" meant the target was on the fourth floor. "Four east" or "four west" would designate specific corridors.

Korda would direct sniper and perimeter team activity based on communications from the team leaders. They would stand by until needed for backup or until the hostage situation required sniper action. Kennedy was on the yellow team, and I was on green. We were second in and starting our search on the second floor. Only my twenty-plus years of training kept me from ditching my team and going directly to the top floor. I was certain he was up there. I could feel him. I couldn't get a bead on Georgia. I prayed that didn't mean she was dead.

It took forever for us to clear the floor. Each bathroom stall and office had to be searched. The sound of boots and the clank of gear were deafening. Entries are only silent in the movies. If anyone else was in this building, they knew we were coming. We moved to the fourth floor and found evidence of squatters but no live inhabitants. As we ascended the stairs, we heard "six west." Either the bad guy or Georgia had been discovered. Every team was on a dead run now for the Armory's sixth floor. My submachine gun had begun to feel heavy, but I was careful not to point it at my hut-hut teammates. We lined up on both sides of the sixth floor door, waiting for the nod from our team leader. When he gave the order, we pushed ahead to assist the sixth floor team. No shots had been fired. A part of me wanted them to save me the shot. As we moved forward, we heard the "all clear" announced on the radio. I watched my teammates stand from their crouches as my mind processed the all clear. *How the hell can it be all clear?* Everyone stood aside as I walked to the westernmost room of the sixth floor. Kennedy waited for me at the entrance to a large room facing the Rose Garden. Standing near the window just outside of the sunlight was a tall figure. My mind tried to identify the figure as Georgia, and yet I dreaded finding her posed like that. As I approached, it became clear the figure was not Georgia but a manikin wearing a veil. No dress. Just a veil and a bouquet of flowers held in its right hand near its chest. The room smelled of bleach and cleaner near the lakeside windows. I heard a "Snipers stand down" command in my ear bud, and someone who had been holding me back released me, allowing me to move forward. In the manikin's left hand was a note clearly intended for me: "You should have come alone. This is between you and me. You're going to have to do better to get Georgia back. You don't deserve her."

I walked over to the window and looked down on the Rose Garden. The bastard had been watching us for so long. How stupid were we? At that moment, I felt hopeless to "do better." How could he anticipate my moves so well while I seemed to be moving in quicksand? I knew that action is much quicker than reaction, but I was so frustrated at my reaction time. I turned to Kennedy.

"How can we get ahead of this guy?"

"How indeed?" was her reply.

I resisted the overpowering urge to lash out at her. She was supposed to have answers. She saw the quick flash of anger in my eyes and stepped back, leaving me to my view of the Rose Garden.

"I'll update my profile. This gives me something more to work with." She wasn't apologizing, just recalibrating her approach. I, on the other hand, was suddenly filled with paranoia. This guy seemed to know my every move.

"Could he be tracking me through my phone?" I asked.

"It's possible. We should issue you a new one to be on the safe side. I think Smitty needs to go over your phone with a fine-toothed comb."

The crime scene team went to work, and I sent Smitty to check on the ownership and tax history of the Armory building. We needed to pull every string on this lead just in case the abductor had screwed up somewhere. I wasn't counting on it, but I wasn't about to cut corners, either.

When I got back to the station, Kennedy handed me a cup of hot chocolate. I sat at my desk, put my feet up, and before I knew it, I had slept for four hours. When I woke up, I felt groggy. An officer who had been sitting in my office watching over me got up when Kennedy came in.

"I drugged you."

I looked at her, stunned. "What the hell?"

"You needed sleep."

"You do that again, and I'll have your badge. I mean it. I need to trust you, and I sure as hell don't have time to sleep right now!"

"I had your back."

"Like hell you did."

She ignored my comment and moved on with no further reference to my nap. "Here's where things are at. I interviewed the technology guy at News 7 to see who would have had access to the interview Genevieve did with you—the one where she straightened your collar."

"And?"

"They did have a security breach roughly six months ago. Someone hacked into their mainframe. They used what resources they had but couldn't track down the hacker. Our FBI central office will dig into it. From what they told me, whoever did it has a lot of skill."

She went on. "Smitty ran the tax records of the old Armory building and came up with another possible lead." She had my attention. "The Armory belongs to the Gant family. It went tax forfeit five years ago, and the Gants were high bidders. The patriarch of the family, Frederico Gant, owns Gant Foods. His plan was to eventually turn the building into a local food production plant. On the surface, it looks like a straightforward business venture, like they were just trying to grow the franchise." She paused.

"On the surface?" I moved my hand in a circle, impatiently waving her on.

"Gant Junior isn't so well respected in the industry. He wants the money and prestige he grew up with, but he's known for taking shortcuts. He has some drug ties. Your guys in the Drug Task Force think he's a mid-level dealer, but they haven't gotten anyone to turn on him yet."

"And this is relevant how?"

"He's got a reputation as a freak with women. He's a bit of a lounge lizard. There are allegations that he has used date rape drugs to take advantage of not-so-willing dates."

My pulse picked up a bit in spite of coming out of my drug-induced slumber. I found that ironic. "Can we pick him up?"

"We're tracking him down now. Daddy isn't talking, but we know where he lives and we've staked out his residence."

"Covert or overt surveillance?" I probed.

"Covert. We have a fake cable TV van parked on the block."

"The killer wants to engage with me. I don't want anyone screwing this up."

"Don't go all Rambo on me."

"You're one to talk." I pointed to the hot chocolate mug. "Beware of profilers bearing gifts. Anything on my phone?"

"No, but we cloned you a clean one anyway, just in case our perp is smarter than Smitty. We did find a tracking device on your car, though. And we found something interesting on Georgia's key ring, a small transmitter embedded in a key. It's a dummy key, one she mistook as her own. We left the tracking device on your car. I've had an officer driving it all over town. I didn't want the killer to know you were at the station. I'm guessing he thinks you've gone rogue and are out searching in vain."

"Anything else?"

"I don't want to scare you, but I assigned a cop to cover Alex. He's the only other vulnerability you have right now, and chances are this guy knows it. I don't even remotely think your son is a target, but I'd rather be safe than wish we had done it later."

"You're right. Thanks."

"When we do pick up Gant Junior, I'll need to bring in a lie expert."

"I need to be the one questioning him," I insisted.

"Oh, you'll get your crack at him. I'm going to have lots to analyze, and so will the lie guy."

The lie guy turned out to be St. Louis County Sheriff's Deputy Michael King. The FBI called him in on a regular basis. An average looking, nondescript kind of guy, he could blend into a party so well that no one would remember he had even been there. If you did notice him, though, you'd see him watching people like teens watch their first R-rated movie.

He and Kennedy were obviously kindred spirits in studying

all things human, kind of like Georgia. That thought sent a wave of grief through me. I sunk to a chair and held my face in my hands, willing it to pass. My heart and soul felt heavy. I pushed everything down except a slow burning rage that I hoped to unleash at the monster who had my Georgia. If Gant was the monster, and we brought him in for questioning and couldn't hold him, I'd blow my only chance. Sure, we could put a tail on him, but what if we lost him? I couldn't stand the thought. Pulling him in might be our only way of getting closer to her.

I expressed my fears to Kennedy. She listened thoughtfully.

"I think our best move is to set up a meet between the two of you. That's assuming he doesn't figure out a way to lure you to him. If that happens, you need to trust me and not go off on your own. We need to make him think you're coming alone, when really you'll be there with major backup."

She cautioned me, "It's a big *if* that Gant is our guy. The killer seems way too smart to leave such a bright crumb trail. The Armory led us right to him."

"I agree, but we have to fully explore this."

"True."

"Okay, but our first priority is to track him down," I said.

"Done."

Nothing, and I mean nothing, happened for the next couple of hours. We assigned squads to surveil Gant's home, known hangouts, and his parent's house. The CSI team came up with zip from the Armory evidence processing, and the note left for me provided no useful clues. I paced and drank coffee and paced some more.

Andrea had not made any progress toward regaining consciousness, but she was still alive, albeit in critical condition.

Smitty found me in the bullpen area and said, "I have something."

"What?"

"I hacked into Gant's Facebook account."

"Do I want to know how?"

"No, and nothing we get is admissible, but I think we can use it."

He pulled up the site. Gant's posts were a brag book about his cars, women, and money. Smitty pointed to the screen. "See here. This is a timeline. He has a habit of checking in wherever he is. The day our first victim went missing, he checked in at home in the morning, off to work with dear old dad, then to the gym at five, followed by dinner and drinks at the Sports Garden until 1a.m." He moved the mouse cursor to another date on the timeline.

"This is the day Georgia went missing. See here?" He pointed with his index finger. "He started out his day at work, then out to lunch at O'Toole's Bar downtown, then to the gym again at five."

"Georgia went missing at 7:30 a.m. This tells us nothing," I said with some anger. I really wanted this to be definitive one way or another.

"Okay. Look at this. Here's why we can't find him. He checked in at the airport at six yesterday morning, and he says he's in Manhattan right now. See the picture of him in front of Times Square?"

"Can this be faked?" I demanded.

"Sure, anything can be faked. But each digital picture has a time stamp on it, and where it was taken is obvious unless steps are taken to hide that. You can't make a picture say it was taken from a different location. Well, not the embedded part."

"Here, I'll show you. Let me try to check in somewhere other than where we are. No. It won't let me unless I create a new place, and then it will show where I actually am."

"What about with a cloned phone?"

"Same thing."

"Could they change the time on the phone to make it work?"

"No. Facebook will imprint the correct time."

"Is he in Manhattan right now or not?" I needed answers, not speculation.

"I don't know. I would need to see his phone or computer to tell you that for sure."

"But anyone could check in as him with this phone, right?"

"Right." He conceded. "Don't you think, though, that if he was trying to set up an alibi, he would have nailed down a better one?" Smitty asked.

I nodded solemnly. It was looking like our big lead was a clear frame-up. It was all too neat. It would take time, but there had to be a solid trail of him being in New York.

"Well, unless he's working with someone, this isn't our guy. Will you give Kennedy the update?"

"Is she going to be okay with me hacking Gant's account?"

"I don't fucking care. Leave that part out." I was coming un-stitched, one seam at a time, and I could both see and feel it happening. Morning was approaching, and Georgia had been missing for nearly twenty-four hours. A lot could happen in twenty-four hours. I paced and pictured Georgia in happier times. My mind would then jump to the picture of her bound by her captor. I couldn't possibly go on, but I couldn't stop, ei-ther. I walked over to the punching bag, gloved up, and let off some steam. As I pounded, I decided there had to be a con-nection to Gant Junior. At least enough of a connection to set him up as a potential suspect. Someone who knew about his management of the building. Someone who'd been in the Armory. I ran to find Kennedy and let her know about my suspicions. She thought I was pulling on a logical string and suggested I bring Smitty up to speed. Since he was sifting through the Facebook data, he could watch for any mention of the Armory or any unusual postings by his friends.

Smitty supported the idea of mining the friends for posts about the building, and he and Corey pulled in a couple of geeks from the lab to help. He laughed at my offer to join in, and told me to keep punching the bag.

Interrogation

Chapter 21

You can only hit a punching bag for so long before your arms give out, your hands get bruised or stress fractured, or you just plain burn out of it. I wandered over to the call line, where Kennedy had been running down leads. We had our crew doing follow-up phone interviews, door knocking, and digging into case files if the callers were or had been on probation, parole, or had served time in a Minnesota prison. The collaboration among the many loosely related law enforcement agencies was impressive.

Kennedy's level of organization was also impressive. She hadn't taken a single note on the effort, but she confessed to me that she did have a recording device on her smart phone so that she could dictate key details. These were being transmitted back to her home office, where a clerical was transcribing the information. Kennedy then delegated follow-up to members of our team. Once they completed a task, they sent their findings via email if it was a dead end, and saw or called her in person if a lead developed. Ninety-nine percent of the calls led nowhere, and it was obscenely time consuming, but in some investigations, a call or tip leads to a viable suspect. The public had been made aware that we were looking for a white male aged twenty-five to forty-five who had issues with marriage and was into power and control, with a law enforcement or military background. The calls were coming in.

Smitty walked in. "Gant is back."

"Where?" I perked up.

"Plane just hit the tarmac. He updated on Facebook as soon as the wheels hit the ground."

Smitty got a call from an officer at the airport. Customs did a "random" search and produced some dope in his luggage. They plucked him right out of the baggage claim area, and he was on his way to the PD.

"We need to bring him in for questioning, but I suspect he's not going to be cooperative." I had a feeling that we were grasping at straws, but he is all we had right now that could possibly lead us to the killer. Somebody let our killer use the Armory, and Gant probably knows who.

It seemed to take forever to bring him in, and I was anxious. Then, after only thirty minutes, the detectives arrived with Gant in cuffs.

He was seated in a fully wired, three-way glass interview room, and I was chomping at the bit to get in there and talk to him. Michael, the St. Louis County Sheriff's office lie guy, and Kennedy were all set to observe from the other side of the glass, and I would sweat him in the interview. If a good cop was needed, Kennedy would come in. We agreed ahead of time to go at him hot. Don't let him get comfortable, and don't treat him like he's innocent. I liked the plan but was concerned about how edgy I felt. I had serious beard growth from a lack of grooming time, and I felt rough.

He looked smug and irritated when I walked in.

I read Gant his rights per Miranda. He agreed to talk with us. They always do when they want to know what we know. Gant was curious about whether we had more than the drug charge, and lawyering-up wouldn't satisfy his urge to know.

"Detail your whereabouts for the past forty-eight hours."

"Excuse me?" he said in a tone that showed he was used to being coddled.

I slammed my fist down on the table. "I'm not screwing around here. Time is short. Tell me your travels for the last forty-eight hours. No, make that three days."

"I've been in New York the last two."

"Why?"

"Vacation. Look, I don't have to tell you anything. What's this all about?"

He wanted to appear innocent and maybe even be liked by the person interviewing him. I wasn't prepared to play that game right now. This was about Georgia.

"It's all about murder, kidnapping, and as long a list of charges as I can come up with." I leaned down in his face, hoping my breath was as bad as I thought it was.

"Maybe I do need a lawyer?" He looked scared.

Kennedy came in, placed a hand on my shoulder, and said, "Let's just slow down and not push too hard here. This is just a guy we're talking to, trying to see what he might know and how he can help us."

"Help you with what?" Gant said.

"Look, if you're innocent, you have nothing to worry about. What did you do leading up to your trip?" Kennedy asked calmly.

"I went to work, the gym, and out to eat. What I always do."

"When is the last time you spent any time at the old Armory?" I asked.

"I haven't been there in six months. Why?"

"I'm asking the questions here." I moved around behind him, wanting him to feel the vulnerability of having me behind his back. "Have you sublet it to anyone?"

"No."

"Lent it to anyone?"

"No. Why?"

"Used it for any legal or illegal purposes in the past year?"

"It's just sitting there. We have plans to eventually use it to expand our food processing operations, but the zoning is tied up at City Hall."

"Have you had any break-ins?" I leaned down into the side of his face from behind.

"Not that I'm aware of. You might want to check with my father. You find someone dead in there or what?"

"Who manages the business?"

"He's transitioning it to me."

"So in the last few months, who's been responsible for it?"

"We both are, but he would know more than me about anyone renting it. Did something happen there?"

"Have you let any of your friends use it?"

"No."

I came in front of him and slammed my fist down again before grabbing him by his shirt and lifting him off of his chair. "What about your drug-dealing friends?" I was pissed off, and it showed.

"I don't have to talk to you." Once his butt hit the seat again, he crossed his arms.

Kennedy cut me off. "Look, Striker. Let's all calm down. Mr. Gant is not under arrest, and I'm sure he doesn't appreciate being manhandled. Let's do this in a more civilized manner, shall we?"

"I don't have time for this," I said and exited the room. I watched as she slowly and methodically built a level of trust and respect with the sleaze bag. In the end, he didn't appear to have a clue who might have had access to the property. The whole interview seemed like a supreme waste of time, and I understood in a real way how some cops lose control and become violent with suspects.

At the conclusion of Kennedy's interview, Michael's take on it was that Gant was indeed dealing drugs, didn't know who had access to the building, but any number of his sleazy friends who were peripherally involved in dealing for him may have had access.

I went back in a second time and pushed him hard on the drugs. "It's only for personal use." Beads of sweat sprung up on his forehead.

"What's for personal use?" I was going to make him tell me.

He turned a shade of red before answering. "Viagra and cocaine."

I didn't respond to him and simply read from the officer's report: "We found 180 pills of Viagra and a kilo of coke. This is a lot of personal use."

He shrugged in silence. "I want a lawyer."

"Daddy's money isn't going to get you out of this." I leaned into him. "You might be able to help yourself, though."

"Lawyer," he repeated.

"Hold him on suspicion of drug trafficking. He traveled across state lines with this. I'll call the prosecutor and ask him to refer this to Federal Court. We'll make a possible link to the murder, and he'll have a high enough bail that his father will think twice about paying. Question him daily. I don't care about the drug charges. I need to find a murderer." I glanced over my shoulder at him as I had him taken away in handcuffs, hoping this might jog his memory about who might have a connection to the warehouse.

The Meeting

Chapter 22

Sergeant Roy headed the Drug Task Force. I knew him and knew of his good work. The average citizen would mistake him for a low-life gang member. He wore loose jeans and a tilted baseball cap, and he looked to be strung out all the time. I often wondered how many of the Task Force guys were active addicts themselves or if they avoided the stuff at all costs. Roy clearly avoided the stuff at all costs. Occasionally he would use the tip of his finger to taste a sample of the drug, but he never went beyond that to convince would-be dealers that he was legit. His boyish looks usually gave him the authenticity he needed to facilitate a controlled buy. I'm sure he didn't have to shave, and that was impressive in a weird sort of way because I'm pretty sure he was in his early thirties. He drove a beat-up old Mustang that had dents and rust but a fast engine.

He was none too happy that we had tipped Gant off that we knew about his involvement in the drug-dealing culture.

"These are the guys who are the hardest to nail. We have to build a case—and it sometimes takes over a year. We've been waiting to arrest the whole web of dealers until we could conclusively link enough of them to Gant to make it stick. You just jeopardized over six months of buys, and roughly three hundred thousand dollars of investment. What made you think you could do this without checking with me?"

I got close to his face and said quietly, "They have my girl-friend. I don't give a rat's ass about your drug deal." I almost spit at him.

Kennedy came between us and said to Roy, "He's out of line, and I'm truly sorry about that," before pulling me out of the room.

"Striker, you're not helping," Kennedy said.

I felt my mind moving very slowly as I tried to focus on her eyes. "No. I'm not."

"You need to get a grip!"

I shrugged. I wanted to pound something or someone. The next person to get in my way was in for a rough time of it, one way or another. I admired the courage it took for her to stay in my line of fire.

"Come on. We're going to get something to eat." She grabbed a staff sergeant and asked him to call her if anything promising came in. We walked three blocks to a mom and pop café on Superior Street, where she ordered a pot roast special for me. We sat in silence for a minute or two before the waitress brought a basket of bread. I felt a little bit of sanity edge back into my conscious mind as I devoured that piece of bread. I hadn't slept or eaten enough, and my last nerve was nearly gone.

"Talk to me," she pushed.

"Georgia is out there, but I can't feel her. I'm scared." I felt my eyes tear up. I didn't bother to wipe them. I sat there, letting a wave of emotions rush through me. Kennedy let me. I felt like my chest was opening right up, and it was jam-packed with pain and sorrow. Kennedy let me sit with it for a few minutes before she gently touched my arm.

"I think she's still alive. I'm nearly certain of it."

I bolted upright. "I'm listening."

"This is more about you now than about Georgia. He's making you sweat. He'll contact you, and then it'll come down to you against him." She paused to make sure I was following. I felt a swell of hope because I knew that she was speaking the truth.

"Unless I've screwed this up somehow already, missed something big," I said.

"I don't think so. This is driving him. He won't let it go until the two of you face off."

As I was considering that possibility, I sensed someone approach from the restaurant entrance. The lieutenant walked to our table in his all-business mode. "Striker, I need to see you in my office."

"We're a little busy here."

"Now!"

"I'm trying to get things done, and time is ticking. What the hell do you want? Sir?"

He paused long enough for Kennedy to get up from the table. She obviously wanted us to step outside.

"I just learned you're in way deeper than I thought."

"Georgia is my world. That hasn't been a secret."

"Yeah, but I didn't know about your connection to our second victim."

"All three, sir! It couldn't be more obvious. He's targeting me. That's why nobody can chase this better than I can."

A lump formed in my throat, and I wasn't even concerned about whether he could see right through me. On some level, I knew that his intervention needed to happen. I was a train that couldn't even remember what a track was, let alone how to stop.

"Dexter, I'm not saying anyone can do it better than you. I'm saying we have people who can do it just as well, and those people don't have the connection."

"Are you kidding me? I mean, with all due respect, sir, I am knee-deep in this, and we can't afford the time it would take to bring someone else up to speed. Don't do this! You could derail the whole investigation and take the steam right out of any advantage we have." I had raised my voice, and people were staring. Kennedy put a hand on me to calm me a bit, and I nearly exploded at her.

Lieu replied in a cold and controlled voice, "What I do know, Mister Insubordinate, is that I want this son of a bitch as badly as you do, and I'm not going to have him go free when it comes out at trial that my lead investigator slept with not one, but two, of the victims." The whole restaurant breathed a collective breath and held it for the next sentence. I hoped to hell no reporters were in the room.

"Are you taking my shield?"

"No. I'm taking you off the case. You're too close, and it's for your own good. Someday you'll thank me."

"Thank you for messing up our chances of stopping this monster?" I knew he was right, but something inside of me wouldn't back down.

"That's enough! Don't sabotage your career, Dexter. Hold your head up, and walk out the door knowing we're doing everything we can. Get out of here, and do something productive."

"Yes, sir," I said with a mock salute. He was right, and I

knew it, but that didn't make it feel any better. I fought the sting of anger that made me want to lash out at him or anyone within striking distance.

"And Striker?"

I couldn't answer him. The best I could do was to glare at him.

"Keep your cell close. I'll keep you in the loop. You have my word."

I left then and started walking toward the cop shop. I wondered what the hell I was going to do. He had ordered me to "do something productive." Did he expect me to go sit on traffic patrol while the rest of the force tracked down the monster who had Georgia?

In the police locker room, the classic stages of grief set in. Denial, as I said to myself that didn't just happen. And anger, as I slammed my fist into my locker and felt the rage rising to the surface.

I had thought I was alone, but a rookie peered around the corner.

"You okay, sir?" he inquired in the deepest voice he could conjure up.

Shit, I thought, I've got to pull it together, or I'm going to give Lieu the confirmation he needs to put me on administrative leave. "I'm fine, just fine." I took a couple of deep breaths.

As I thought about what to do next, I longed for Georgia. I was spinning out of control. *Where is my zone?* I headed to the showers before someone else could see me teetering on the edge. As I stepped into the tiny, tiled shower, I began to shake. *What the hell is happening to me? More important, what is happening to Georgia? Son of a bitch! Where are you, you fucking monster?*

I stayed in the shower and decided I needed some distance

from headquarters while I decided how to go after the killer on my own. The lieutenant was forcing me to go rogue, and at this point, my career meant nothing. Georgia was more important than anything else.

A few minutes later, I walked up to my desk. Across the way, Kennedy and Smitty were going over documents.

"What's up?" Smitty asked. Kennedy's glance to the floor immediately confirmed for me that she had been the one to drop a dime on the Lieu.

I looked right at her. "You think I'm too close? I thought we were working to find this son of a bitch together! Don't you care?"

"I do, Striker. I do."

In shock, Smitty stared at her and then back at me, looking bewildered. "Striker, they took you off the case?"

I continued to glare at Kennedy "Yes, sir. Apparently I'm too involved and can't keep my head clear."

Smitty looked at me like a lost kid. "What are you going to do, boss?"

"I'm going for a drive." I grabbed my extra cuffs from the top drawer of my desk and shoved them in my pocket, heading for the garage.

I signed out my favorite maroon smooth-top; performed the required checks on the lights, radar, and standard equipment; and hit the road. God, it felt good to be at the helm of a purpose-built, responsive machine. It seemed to anticipate what I wanted it to do and made me feel like I had some control. I headed south of Duluth and brought her up to cruising speed in the inside lane along the grass strip that separated north from south lanes, drove in and out of Duluth, crisscrossing the city several times.

I was in the mode, but more important, my mind was sharp. I had every case fact running through my mind in vivid detail.

What had I missed? Where's he at now? What's his next move? What's this all about? Then I got a cold dose of reality: *How is Georgia? I'm thinking things are bad for me, but what is she going through? She's a fighter! She's alive, and I know it!*

My cell rang and snapped me out of my mental gymnastics. I answered, "Striker."

"Lieu here. I know I ordered you out of this, but we need you back here now."

"What's up?" I had a sinking feeling that things had taken a turn for the worse.

"He sent a note to you here at the PD. We opened it, and he's demanding to see you, alone, at the antenna farm. I can't see a way to keep you out. I need you, not as the lead investigator, but to find out what he wants, give us a way to get to him. We'll wire you up and have the area covered with snipes."

I grabbed some grass, headed north, and let the ponies run toward Duluth.

I needed to meet this lunatic at the antenna farm above Duluth at 10 p.m., unarmed, in only thirty minutes. Part of me just wanted to see him, under any conditions. I changed into street clothes and was rigged with a wire and a code word to summon the cavalry. They didn't let me in on the plan, but the tactical commander assigned was Korda and I knew his style. He'd blanket the area with snipers and observers equipped with night vision scopes. They'd lie low and not be detected by the perp. I didn't know Korda's exact plan, but I knew his pet peeve, cross fire. He'd have his guns high aimed downhill, downrange. I was confident they wouldn't be detected, and if I needed them, they'd be there before I asked.

After the nerds wired me, I was ready. On the way out, I checked the view in the mirror. There was no sign of anyone trailing me. I felt naked without my .380, so I tucked it into my pocket so that I could at least stash it in the car. The irony of my gun fixation and that I was going into the most dangerous and high-stakes situation of my life without it was not lost on me.

Smitty's voice crackled into my earpiece: "We're ready, boss. I have a good feeling."

"Shut up, Smitty. Just shut the hell up." My breathing was rapid as I turned down the goat path that led to the antenna farm. I knew he was here. I sensed him. I felt something else, too, and hoped it was Georgia. I used my peripheral vision to check the spots I would have set up in if I were doing backup. Nothing. Korda's boys were the best.

I parked the car just past the gate and walked the rest of the way in. I stood on the hill perched nine hundred feet above the city. This crest was once the shore of a great lake long, long ago. Actually back in the Stone Ages. *What did it look like back then? What creatures frequented this shoreline? What threatened them?* I sprang back to the moment and spun around to the north in reaction to hearing a twig snap. I was aware I was unarmed, but my senses were on high alert. Like all cops, I am a master of assessing danger and reacting quickly. In this case, it was a deer.

I turned back to the skyline, and my cell rang. Swiping it, I saw a 404 area code I knew to be from a prepaid phone. As I positioned the cell to my ear, I heard a smoky voice laughing. "What the hell is so funny?"

"You jumping at that deer!"

I scanned the darkness for any sign. Clearly he was here.

My earpiece came back on: "Striker. Lieu. We can't hear him. He's got it scrambled, and we're in the dark. Advise."

The smoky voice continued: "Don't bother looking. She's not here with us. She's at the mansion. See you there. You'll wear a tux. I've stashed one at the 7-Eleven on

Eighteenth and Superior Street. Don't bother asking about who dropped it off—I had a courier arrange everything. I used your credit card, so it's top of the line. Oh, and leave your buddies behind if you ever want to see our sweetie alive."

The voice was vaguely familiar, and it wasn't Smitty. *Maybe he was disguising his voice. How could he pull that off?* "Our sweetie." *What the hell did that mean. Who is this guy?* I didn't have the luxury of time to ponder this.

"Advise, Striker. I heard mansion and that's it. Advise, God damn it!" It was Smitty. I stripped the earpiece and tracker from my chest and ran. I ran as fast as I could toward the darkness that concealed the edge of the steep hill. I knew there would be confusion with the team. There'd be a delay, but it wouldn't be long.

I ran over the edge of the hill and down the steep embankment. I tripped over brush and was smacked by branch after branch as I crashed down the hill. Running as fast as I could, I managed to keep my feet underneath me as I progressed down the steep bank. A few hundred feet down, I ran over an edge and came to the realization that I was falling. The drop-off was only a few fee, but it was enough to make me roll uncontrollably. I was still headed down. Down and away from the team but toward where I needed to be to save Georgia.

I came to a flat area that was clearly an alley. I made my way between two houses and headed toward Skyline Parkway. I was a long way from the antenna farm by road but I assumed at least a portion of the team was going to be coming down that hill, and I needed separation. I needed it now. Headlights came from the west, and I saw the white arch on the roof identifying the car as a Town Taxi. I stepped into its path. The cab screeched to a halt. I approached the passenger side and opened the front door of the cab. As I sat down, a frog-voiced woman in her fifties told me that company policy required passengers to ride in the back. I reached across her and opened the driver's door. "It's my cab now, and my policy is to ride alone." I gave her a shove, and the discussion was over. As she hit the pavement, I slammed the car in gear and stabbed the gas. I sped away as the driver waved furiously in the rearview.

When he had said "the mansion", I had no idea what he was talking about. In Duluth, there are a hundred mansions, but the most notably Glensheen. Everybody knows the place, especially cops. It had been the location of a dramatic murder and yet remained a hot spot for weddings. First I had to get to the tux, and I presumed the next clue waited for me there.

Preparation

Chapter 23

I had no time to formulate a plan. He had likely fitted the tux tight so that he could see a shoulder holster bulge, which didn't matter because my gun was back at the antenna farm in my car. So much was riding on this. My skin crawled, aching for Georgia. Memories of holding her flooded me. I worried that he had already set up cameras throughout Glensheen. God I hoped it was Glensheen. So much was riding on it being Glensheen. Given the travel and the time it was taking me to pick up the tux, he had plenty of time to prep. *Damn. It has to be Glensheen.* The site of one of Duluth's most well-known murders—one that had inspired a bestselling novel written by the lead investigator and prosecutor who had documented the murder of the heiress to the Congdon family fortune as well as her nurse. The mansion was now owned by the local university and was run as a tourist attraction. I worried about everything, fighting fear-induced paralysis.

I can do this, I thought. *I have to.*

Semi-rested and having eaten, I wasn't nearly as strung out. I took a couple of deep breaths.

A tux. I knew that the scene he was constructing was somehow going to be a duel for Georgia followed by a wedding. The fantasy might mean that he had not yet assaulted her. She had to be alive. I focused on her strength and her martial arts training. But I was still horrified and worried about how he was treating her. Even if I succeeded in saving her life, how would she overcome the trauma of this ordeal?

I knew from my work in training on domestic violence how men who batter women think about them. What drives them to abuse is thinking that they're better than women. More powerful. That it's their right and privilege to control the women they abuse or stalk. Most crimes against women have those exact origins. I made a promise to God that if I could get Georgia out of this alive and relatively healthy, I would redouble my efforts to train cops about domestic violence. I'd work harder to educate men and our city about the screwed-up thinking that permeates our culture about women and children as property.

I ditched the cab a block from the Holiday Mall and hopped a bus the rest of the way to the 7-Eleven, knowing that Georgia's well-being depended on me arriving without a police escort. I had to evade my team while following the killer's instructions to the letter. As I made the short bus ride, I pondered my old cases scouring my memory banks for anyone in my past who might want to settle a score with me. Who had I wronged or competed with over a woman? I came up blank in the five-minute ride. I got off the bus two blocks past my destination and made my way slowly back so

I wouldn't draw unnecessary attention to myself. I was now on the run from the law.

At the 7-Eleven, I approached the teenaged clerk. "Do you have a package for me? I'm Dexter."

"Yeah, we usually don't get requests like this, but for a fifty-dollar tip—hell, I'll take these deliveries any time," the pimply faced teen said with enthusiasm.

I didn't bother telling him that a murderer had made the arrangements in my name, using my credit card. The monster was deep inside my life, pulling the strings in a hideous puppet show. It both infuriated me and deepened my sense of helplessness.

Changing hurriedly into the tux in the men's room, I didn't bother looking in the mirror to see what I looked like. As I jogged down to the bus stop, I went over my recollection of Glensheen and potential access and entrance points. The estate was bordered by Lake Superior to the south, a cemetery to the west, a buffer of woods to the east separating it from another smaller mansion, and busy London Road to the north. The property was roughly seven acres, which is unheard of inside the city limits, and which would make my mission considerably more difficult.

Another problem was the encroaching darkness. I let the danger settle into my bones and brought my surroundings into sharp focus. The stakes would never be higher, so I steeled myself for the encounter of my life. I was determined to bring Georgia home.

Alone

Chapter 24

On foot, I crossed London Road bordering Lake Superior to the Glensheen estate, walking alone onto the land. I reached for my gun, but it wasn't there. The one thing that centered me all day every day, let alone when facing a life or death showdown, wasn't there. I was beyond the irony of that now, and it freed me in some bizarre way. Now I had to reach deep within to find my strength. It didn't lie anywhere external. What centered me now had nothing to do with self-preservation. I had feelings for Georgia that I had never experienced before. In actuality, I had felt them but pushed them aside. I was a champion at not letting anyone get too close. Now I realized, she is my center. I would do anything for her, even if it hurt me or showed my weaknesses. I wondered if I had done that for Alex.

More importantly, had I taught him that was part of being a grown up?

The sun had dipped below the horizon, the sky a thin line of deep pink to the west. My heart beat a steady, sure rhythm in my chest, and I took several centering breaths, finding the steely place that allowed my focus to fine-tune. I could almost feel Georgia doing the same. I let no doubt creep in. Whatever happened, I would read it and respond. I willed that strength for Georgia, too. This was it.

I entered the grounds from the west through the graveyard. Shaking off the foreboding feeling of death that permeated the air, I vaulted over the fence and walked confidently along the border of the property to the lake, where I jumped yet another fence. The century-old Glensheen estate lay peaceful and removed from the modern world. I felt death there, too. A garden path wound its way in front of the lake and through several patio areas commonly used for weddings. The lights from the lift bridge twinkled magically over the lake to the west as did a soft glow from the lights of a ship awaiting entry into the harbor. I could see what drew people to Glensheen for weddings. It was a romantic setting. The general public didn't know or had forgotten the intimate details about the gruesome murders that took place at Glensheen in 1977. As a detective, I was haunted by them and hoped Georgia wasn't going to be the next victim at the mansion.

The phone signal had been garbled enough when I received the meet location that Kennedy and the crew wouldn't be on top of us too quickly. I followed the path through the estate, mapping the layout in my mind—the main house, the outbuildings, including carriage and boat houses. The killer could easily see that I had arrived. I walked up and onto the back patio of the main house and then back down to the central garden where I stood, motionless, listening, careful not to touch where my weapon would be if I had one.

The main house was a thirty-nine-room brick mass that seemed to absorb everything nearby like a black hole. I fought its pull because another intuition was telling me this would not happen in the main house. I tuned all of my senses into my surroundings. I could feel him near. I sensed Georgia, too, and knew that she was alive. The air smelled of freshly cut grass and the gardens. My mind flashed to the smell of roses and the initial scene when I first spotted Genevieve bizarrely posed under the wedding arch. The hair on my whole body stood on end.

In my peripheral vision, I saw a red flashing light hanging from a tree toward the lake. I quickly moved to it. It appeared to be some kind of a homing beacon. Plucking it from the branch, I held it in my hand, watching its red pulsating light flash slowly. Its speed didn't change as I waved it around, so I began walking toward the mansion. The pulsing light slowed. I turned and walked toward the lake, and the flashing picked up speed. Making my way toward the lower gardens, I honed my senses to everything around me. I had traveled roughly two hundred feet, midway to the lake and rocky beach, when the light began to pulse slower, so I backtracked to the faster pulse. I looked to my left and saw a garden shed one hundred feet away. As I moved toward it, the light pulse increased. My eyes were adjusting to the darkness, but the red light was interfering with my night vision.

An ornate storybook cottage, the garden shed was likely a child's playhouse at one point. I wondered if the now acquitted daughter of the murdered Elizabeth Congdon had played there as a privileged child. I felt a shiver go through me at the thought of the gruesome and cold-blooded murders that took place in the main house, and now I was about to confront an even colder killer.

As my boot hit the porch of the garden shed, and the red light beat a fast pace, I froze mid-step. I decided to do a perimeter check of the building to look for trip wires. I didn't think the murderer would want the game to be over so swiftly, but I also knew this confrontation would be a complicated match of skill and smarts. Halfway around the building, I was able to see into a window. The small structure was empty except for a package with another blinking light on it.

Now what? I thought. Rather than risk setting off a bomb rigged to be activated by the device in my hand, I threw the strobe light up toward the main building. I then looked into the window again, and the light inside was now flashing at a slower rate. *Okay. The package likely had a bomb inside. Not likely to explode now that I have discarded the triggering device, but I'm not chancing it.*

I continued to walk around the structure until I came to the step again. I noticed an off-colored rock placed among the others in a small rock garden bordering the front steps. I gingerly picked it up. It had a slide-open compartment meant for hiding house keys. Inside was a note, "You will live to see me marry her this night. Weep not for your loss but celebrate our love." I wondered what Kennedy would make of the language in the note. It had a Shakespearian influence. I thought she would say that meant he was educated. Cultured.

I looked around to see only gardens. Shit! No blinking light was going to help me here. It was dark, but a cloud-covered quarter moon bathed the grounds in faint light. I was flying solo. At least I hoped I was, but I imagined a sniper up on the roof of the mansion. I wondered if the killer sensed the same thing. If I was him, I would be down by the lake giving myself protection from sniper fire. Unless, of course, I had been able to secure a boat. Sniper fire from a boat on Lake Superior wasn't a good bet, as the wave action and wind would prohibit a good shot.

I eased down the embankment slowly. It was difficult to do without turning around. Looking out over the water, I couldn't see any boats in close proximity. A ship was moored out in front of the lift bridge a few miles away. The shore consisted of car-sized boulders interspersed with smaller rocks. It was a mild sixty-degree night. Once at lake level, I stood motionless to allow my eyes and ears to tune into my surroundings. I wondered where Kennedy and the rest of the team was. I felt her support. Even though I had abandoned them and gone rogue, I was certain that each and every one of them would have done the same thing. If all went well, I'd probably have my job. If things didn't, I would be done as a cop. But that would mean that I hadn't saved Georgia, and I wouldn't care if I had a job. I shook off any doubt and refocused.

To my left I saw the flicker of another light. *Was it a candle in the boathouse?* I walked gingerly over the uneven surface, contemplating my next move. The boathouse had been meticulously maintained by a maintenance crew. Its wooden exterior boards appeared to have been painted dozens of times over its lifespan. I did a perimeter search that revealed little save the flickering candlelight within. The lake entrance to the structure had been sealed up, but water still moved freely in and out beneath it. The only other entrance was a windowless door that faced west. I threw caution to the wind and tried the doorknob. It turned freely. Before entering, I looked around for anyone else who might be on the grounds. I couldn't see the main house from this vantage point at all, and any boats out in the water that were unlit were invisible to me. I pushed the door open with a deafening creek and stood to the side listening.

"Striker?" Georgia's tentative voice called out.

It took all of my restraint to keep from rushing in.

"Yes, Georgia, it's me. Are you alone? Is it safe for me to come in?" I tried for a conversational voice while my heart pounded in my ears. I should have known this was a setup that I couldn't resist. I remember a vague pang of intuition when I sensed motion behind me, felt a blow to the head, and everything went black.

You Love Him?

Chapter 25

The world was a blur when I tried to pry open my eyes. My head felt like it had been split in half. Two figures took shape in front of me. I couldn't focus, so I closed my eyes again.

A male voice said, "This is your hero, your savior." His tone was mocking.

It was him. The serial killer had Georgia, and now he had me. I opened my eyes again, desperately trying to focus. I couldn't believe what I saw. I blinked a second time, certain my eyes were playing tricks on me. It was Kent Larsen. He too had on a tuxedo, and Georgia was wearing a wedding dress. I looked around to see that we were still in the boathouse. The sound of gently lapping water filled the space, which was lit entirely by a dozen or so candles. The naturally graying cedar walls had been decorated with flowers, and a makeshift wedding arch was adorned with lace. Georgia looked alert and okay, but I was still fuzzy.

"Kent?" I said in disbelief.

"Oh, you disappoint me." He grabbed my shirt and slammed me to the ground. "You aren't so hot shit now, are you?" He spat at me.

I felt stunned by his explosive anger and remained flat on my back. He had the same musky smell that I remembered from the attacker at our home. My head was a throbbing tide of pain. When I didn't respond right away, he seemed to get a hold of himself and stepped back. My hands were tied behind my back, so I had to work to sit up.

I was still gaining focus, and the walls were spinning a little. I blinked several times, trying to see clearly enough to anticipate his actions. Georgia looked stressed, but now that my vision was clearer, I could see that she wasn't drugged. I locked eyes with her and sent her a look that said, "Don't worry, we'll figure this out." I turned my attention back to Kent, the evidence tech, feeling a surge of hope and confidence about being able to gain control of the situation. I flashed back to the image of him sitting in the lab and pretending to work on this case. I found it hard to believe that this nerd was my adversary. I just needed a plan and the right opportunity.

Then I saw a flash in his eyes that chilled me. In that moment, I knew I was dealing with not just a socially awkward "paste eater," but with a strategic and cruel killer. We had underestimated how dangerous he really was, and how deranged.

The boathouse had exposed beams and a deep-water well for boat storage surrounded by decking. No boat was moored there now, though. The opening to the lake had been boarded up to deter neighboring kids and any other trespassers from becoming a liability risk, but ice-cold water in the well lapped up and down with the waves of the lake, chilling the small boathouse.

Georgia surprised me by saying, "You didn't need to come. I'm okay."

At first I was shocked, and then I realized she was playing her part. "What do you mean, I didn't need to come?" I asked her, acting incredulous.

"Kent and I are in love. You don't need to be here."

"What the hell are you saying?" I asked her. Kent watched her for a response.

"I have come to appreciate Kent. He's smart. Capable. I choose him now. You can leave."

"I'm not leaving. This isn't over. We aren't over," I implored. My mind was clearing, and I had a vague sense that Georgia had a plan and was playing him somehow. Playing into his psyche. Georgia had his attention.

Kent stood a little taller and seemed pleased. Finally, a bride fit for his fantasy! I knew Georgia's therapist perceptions would help her to manage his delusions. I didn't want to say something to set him off, so I stayed quiet.

"Kent and I have been getting acquainted. He told me about how you took all the glory for the investigations you worked on together. He does the work, and you get all of the attention. That's not fair. You haven't given him proper credit."

"Excuse me?" I asked without thinking.

"Yes. You abused your position and power." She nodded emphatically, escalating her anger as she spoke, nearly spitting her words. Kent was so happy he began untying her restraints.

"None of you really know him. He's strong, kind, and sensitive. He's transformed himself." He finished untying her, and she stood behind him, placing a hand on his shoulder. "I love him, and there's not a damn thing you or anybody can do about it."

Seeing her in a wedding dress standing next to a serial killer freak in a tux was almost too much for me to take. The bizarre scene made me smile inwardly, though, because Georgia was free from her restraints. He even trusted her enough to turn his back to her.

How was the wedding supposed to play out here? What happened after the wedding? Was he really that out of touch with reality? Was I to be the best man or killed? I wished this script was written. I sensed him watching me for a reaction.

"No. This isn't happening to me," I said dejectedly.

This made him smile. He turned to Georgia. "Prepare our feast. We'll marry at the top of the hour."

I didn't know what time it was. Georgia moved to a table where a cheese and meat spread had been placed. A bottle of champagne and two glasses awaited the final celebration. Clearly the fantasy did not include all three of us hanging around after the wedding. Kent smiled broadly at the wedding arch. I took the time to think about my adversary. He was a cop, as much as any paste eater is a cop, and had worked in electronics in some capacity. His pupils were dilated, so I wondered if he wasn't on a drug of some kind.

I also wondered how Kennedy and the rest of the police were doing in tracking down our location. I was ready for them to join the party. Duluth, especially the neighborhood of Congdon, is littered with mansions from the early mining, shipping, and lumber booms. I was hoping the instincts of my brothers and sisters in blue would bring them to the most notorious mansion of them all, a.k.a. the Congdon Mansion, before this wedding was over.

Make Your Move

Chapter 26

Georgia arranged two plates of food and set them at the makeshift table. "What about him?" she asked. "Should I set a plate for him?"

"What do you think, Striker? Will you be man enough to help us celebrate?" he asked. His speech was a tad too fast, like he had taken amphetamines, or maybe methamphetamines. He was on some kind of speed. I had to think one step ahead of him, but I wasn't sure of the script. If I played along too easily, the whole charade could fall apart. On the other hand, if I objected, we could end up dead. I knew at some point Georgia would make her move. She would try to take him out. My best chance—no, our best chance—was for me to get free from my bonds somehow.

"You ask a lot of me. First you steal my girl, then you want me to stand by you?"

"She has never been your girl," he said with a burst of anger.

Georgia seemed to agree with him. "If you ever cared about me, you would want me to be happy. You'd want the best for me. For us." She stood next to Kent and held his arm.

"All right," I said.

He wore a shoulder holster, and although he didn't draw his weapon, I knew from experience what a comfort he took in its presence. I tried to casually look around for something to use as a weapon. My hands were tied behind my back, but there was a tiny bit of play. I worked them back and forth, trying to stretch the rope.

Georgia had chosen him over me. This was something he couldn't accomplish with his two previous victims. I wondered what it had been like for Genevieve and Andrea. Why had he targeted them? Presumably because he wanted everything I had as well as the glory I'd garnered from solving cases. He even coveted the women I loved. He must have been enraged when he learned that his stalking hadn't endeared him to them.

I decided I needed to keep him talking while I worked my hands free. "Why Genevieve?"

"I saw the way she worshiped you. You didn't do anything to solve that case! Without me, nothing would have happened. No arrest. No interview. No newspaper article. That should have been mine. She should have been mine!" He spat the words at me.

"Why Andrea?" I knew the answer but needed him to keep talking.

"She never would have been attracted to you if it weren't for me. You couldn't solve a grade school math problem. Without my work, you were nothing!" He was right in my face now.

The veins in his neck bulged from his rage, and his hands shook as he pointed a finger at me. As he reached for his pistol, Georgia made her move and kicked him square in the face. He went down hard but was back up quickly. He had his gun halfway out when she kicked again, knocking the gun out of his hand and causing it to clatter to the floor.

I stood up, giving myself a little more wiggle room and found that I could slip one hand halfway out of the tie. My hands were swelling, and I could barely feel them, but I strained even harder.

When Georgia made a move for the gun, Kent slammed her from behind, and she fell awkwardly to the floor in a heap.

I broke free from the ties just as Kent spotted the gun midway between us. I made a lunge for it, but my damaged hand wouldn't close around the weapon. He pushed my hand aside and regained control of the gun.

All three of us jumped as a bullhorn signaled a warning sound before my lieutenant's voice boomed from somewhere outside the boathouse.

"We have you surrounded. Release the hostages, and come out with your hands up."

Kent moved over to a window and stood to the side, trying to see out without getting in the line of fire. He pointed the gun at me. "Don't fucking move an inch, or I'll kill you," he said.

Georgia had slowly stood and was edging toward him while keeping him between us for a strategic advantage.

"It's okay. It's going to be okay," she said to him. I sensed his confusion, partially from Georgia professing her love for him and partially from Georgia's well-placed kick to his head. Kent looked at her trying to figure it all out while she gazed into his eyes convincingly.

"Send one of the hostages out," Lieu yelled into the bullhorn.

"I'm not going," Georgia said firmly.

Was she playing her role or trying to protect me? I wondered.

He had the gun out with his finger on the trigger. I hoped Georgia saw that and wasn't thinking about making another move just then.

"It's ruined. Why did they have to ruin everything?" He waved his gun around, finger still on the trigger.

He slammed his left hand into the side of the building. Braced for a forced entry, I pictured the snipers trained on the building and the arsenal loaded and locked on this tiny boathouse. When nothing happened, I took a deep breath.

"Calm down, man. That could have made them storm the building. You gotta stay calm. Okay?" I implored.

His whole arm twitched, including his trigger finger. I felt a bead of sweat trickle down my back. So many things could go wrong here.

"Let me talk to them. I have someone out there who we can trust. Someone who can understand you. Someone who will make sure we won't get hurt."

"Who?" he said. He looked like his head was hurting. Maybe his high was wearing off.

"Kennedy. She's my friend. She's from the FBI, and she admires your work," Georgia said.

"You can ask for her then." He nodded at Georgia. "Do it. Tell them to back off, or I'll kill the hero."

"I'm going to go to the door. Will I be okay?" she asked me.

"Move slowly. Show them that your hands are empty."

Georgia opened the door, held her palms out first, and then stood openly in the doorway. "I need to talk to Kennedy."

I couldn't see anything but heard Kennedy come on the loudspeaker. "Georgia, are you okay?"

"Yes."

"Is Striker okay?"

"Yes."

"What do you need?" Kennedy was speaking as softly as could be accomplished over a loudspeaker.

"We are in here with Kent Larsen. He's an evidence tech. He's been wronged by everyone. Everyone needs to value his part in investigations."

Kent moved over to me and put his arm around my neck, pulling me into him as a hostage shield. His weapon was lowered by his side, so I ducked down and tried to flip him. All I managed to accomplish was to get out of his grip. Georgia turned around at the commotion and rushed him and me, landing a chest-high kick and sending him sprawling into the wall opposite the door that had swung back closed. As soon as he hit the wall, I rushed him. He side-stepped my attack, sending me head first into the wall. I felt a warm trickle run down into my eyes, and my vision went red.

I heard a shuffle and knew Georgia was going at him with everything she had. When my eyes cleared, I saw that she was down on the ground. He moved the gun to her head. I slammed into him, and we both ended up tumbling onto the ground and into the ice-cold water near the boat entry door. When I came up for air, Larsen had his gun pointed at me. We locked eyes, and he pulled the trigger. Click. Both of us looked at the gun. Did it misfire from being wet, or had Kent forgotten to put one in the chamber? I was so stunned I nearly didn't react. Kent let go of me to grab the slide and rack another round in. I head-butted him and then saw Georgia's foot make contact with his torso as she jumped into the water. I was numb from the forty-degree water temperature of Lake Superior. I held onto one of the mooring posts in an effort to regain and refocus my strength, shivering with my teeth clattering. I watched in slow motion as Kent reached up and pulled Georgia under the water by her foot.

Where's the cavalry now? I thought. As I saw him pull her under, I pushed off the post, got a grip and yanked on his tuxedo jacket trying to hold him under. Georgia was able to break free and scrambled to the side dock where she pulled herself up in spite of the waterlogged wedding dress dragging her down. Kent wiggled from his jacket and came to the surface now free of my grasp. He plotted a course straight toward Georgia moving slower from the cold. As Kent pulled himself out of the water, I saw his hands were empty, and I prayed the gun was on the Lake Superior floor.

They moved in a circle around the boathouse, and she managed to avoid him while I managed to get my frigid muscles to thrust myself up and out of the water. I lunged at him and landed my forearm across his chin with enough force to stun a giant. Kent landed hard on the ground and I was immediately on him. I straddled his chest and grabbed his throat with both hands. Kent looked at me with a minor smirk on his face as I squeezed harder. My grasp was a technique that stopped all blood flow to and from Kent's brain. I trained cops across the nation on the deadliness of this move that was common among domestic violence. Eight seconds and he would be out, and I could feel it working.

As Kent slipped into unconsciousness, I felt my rage and grip increase. My mission was complete, I could easily roll him over and hold his hands in an apprehension hold and call in the forces to make the arrest, but I didn't stop. I held my strangulating grip and continued to look into the eyes of a man who had caused me and those close to me so much pain. The human brain shuts down after about eight seconds with no oxygen and will normally recover quickly if the pressure is released and the carotid arteries are allowed to flow. I knew all too well that maintaining the pressure too long would cause the brain to reach a point of no return and cause certain death. This is exactly why cops stopped using choke holds about a decade ago, but I held it anyway. I squeezed the neck of this now limp body who had left his would-be bride so gruesomely in the Rose Garden. I squeezed as I thought about the suffering he had put Andrea through and I squeezed as I thought about him trying to take everything that meant anything to me.

"Striker" Georgia yelled as she grabbed both sides of my face and looked directly into my eyes. "It's over. You are not the judge and the executioner. You are the cop, the good guy. You stop the evil and apprehend the bad guy. Your job is not to bring justice to the lawless but bring the lawless to justice. You're not a killer. You're better than him. You're better than him."

I released my hold and fell back as Kennedy, who had clearly heard Georgia's words, pushed open the door and trained her gun on Kent.

Kennedy looked past Georgia and Kent directly at me "You okay?" I nodded yes. Kennedy yelled toward the door "We got three survivors in here. Stand down the snipers and get the medics in here." She looked back at me. "You're okay. We're all going to be just fine here."

Georgia rushed to me and we embraced still on the floor against the wall. Kennedy stepped aside from the door and the Lieutenant entered the boathouse. He looked at me with an expression I hadn't seen in a long time. He looked at me like my Father looked at me when I was a young child and had survived being nearly hit by a car while retrieving a ball in the street. His look showed relief that I had survived, but his anger at my decisions, defiance of his direction and assessment of my judgment were apparent. He walked out not saying a word as the medics came in.

"Did he hurt you?" I whispered into her ear.

"No. Thank god."

"You are amazing and I love you more than life itself."

Plea

Chapter 27

Thankfully, Larsen plead guilty to one charge of murder and three counts of attempted murder. The remaining twenty-three charges were dropped in exchange for him being sentenced in the State Court as opposed to the Federal Court. His lawyer had convinced him that the Minnesota prison system was a much more humane way to serve time than in some of the Federal prisons where he would otherwise land. Not even paste-eater cops do well in prison, not when they've had a part in putting many of the inmates away.

The sentencing hearing was on a Tuesday in front of a packed courtroom. Reporters jammed the front of the Court-house, with the Honorable Judge Lambert presiding. She was known for her compassion for victims, strict adherence to the law, and long lectures at sentencing. She was also one of the few judges who wasn't swayed by media attention and public opinion. The media had dubbed Larsen the Groom Killer. He waived his right to a jury and was to be sentenced by Judge Lambert. The pre-sentence investigation and Minnesota Sentencing Guidelines presumptive sentence for all of the charges combined called for a range of between forty-eight and sixty-eight years in prison.

Georgia sat quietly beside me as the judge directed the prosecution and defense to make their oral arguments. She also heard the probation officer's final recommendation. Alex sat on one side of me. Georgia had allowed him to read her statement before the trial, and they had spent a good deal of time talking about why she didn't advocate for the harshest punishment possible. We had submitted victim statements as had the other victims and their families. We were asked if we wanted to make a statement at the hearing, and we reserved that right.

Once the final arguments were made, the judge turned to Georgia. So did the killer. I felt her stiffen beside me, then breathe in and out, composing herself.

"I do wish to be heard, your honor." She stood, composed herself again, and pulled out a piece of paper. The judge motioned toward a podium, and she walked slowly up to it, deliberately looking at Larsen as she walked by him. Because there was no jury, she cleared her throat and spoke directly to the judge.

"Great tragedy brings us here today, your honor. It is not just the impact on me that must be considered, but also the impact on Genevieve, Andrea, those who love and have loved them, and the broader community." She looked at the killer as she composed herself again. She took a moment to summarize her statement in sign language to Alex before continuing. "There is no real justice when a life is brutally taken.

All lives have promise. All lives have value. That can never be undone." She straightened. "I've looked into the sentencing guidelines in an attempt to prepare for this moment, your honor. I've done due diligence to aggravating and mitigating factors, the possibilities of concurrent and consecutive sentencing, and what I have come to, your honor, is that none if it can add up to a life unlived, potential unreached, a shadow of fear cast over a community."

She looked at the judge again. "Your job is not an easy one. To sentence him to anything less than the upper range could depreciate the seriousness of the crimes and have a negative impact on the victims. To sentence a man beyond what could be reasonably determined as rehabilitation is a waste of taxpayer money and also limits his potential. Frankly, the question comes down to redemption. Can someone who has taken a life redeem themselves in the eyes of God? In the eyes of their community? It seems infinitely immeasurable to me from this early vantage point, but yet, that is the conversation we're having." She breathed a heavy sigh.

"I can tell you the impact that this has had on me. It has forever changed how I view humankind and how I view our potential. I've studied the human mind my entire adult life. I thought I understood most of its twists and turns. I even believed I could help most see choices and paths in a clearer light—to help them illuminate their choices. Now I look at my clients who have darker tendencies with a note of fear. Fear of what they could become if left unchecked. It has altered my perception of what harm is possible in the world. Yet I can see this man's humanity. It makes me see him in all of us. In some ways, he's merely a product of so much conditioning. Conditioning that allows men to possess women, to control them. Whatever you do today, Judge, I will move on. Move forward. I will also offer my services to the remaining victims and their families without charge. We will all heal. Not completely, but as completely as we can. Thank you for your time."

She made her way back to me, and I could feel her body shake ever so slightly as she sat beside me. I reached for her hand and gave her a gentle squeeze. Alex gave her a thumbs up.

We heard from several family members of Andrea and Genevieve before Genevieve's father finally stood at the podium. I could see the little vein by his temple pulsing as he tried to compose himself. He had also written a statement. He spoke of Genevieve, who she was as a child, and of her hopes and dreams. He quoted from her poetry and read from a journal about some of the volunteer work she had done. He openly wept as he closed. "I agree with Georgia Frank when she said you have a hard job. None of it will bring back my baby. I would gladly take her place if I could. I, too, will work to help victims of violent crimes. I will work with Ms. Frank to set up a fund to provide counseling to both victims of violence and perpetrators of violent crime who wish to change. I ask that half of this man's prison wages be collected and used for that purpose as well. I ask that he receive the longest sentence allowed. I cannot bear to think about even the slightest possibility that he could take another life. Thank you."

Sentencing

Chapter 28

Judge Lambert took a short recess before pronouncing the sentence. The County Attorney's victim advocate invited us down to wait in the coffee shop. All of the victims and loved ones sat around a huge table and got some of their questions answered about the sentencing process. Most of the questions had to do with the Minnesota Sentencing Guidelines and why murder didn't add up to a life sentence, period. I sympathized with them. Georgia made connections with a couple of people to start a support group.

Once back in the courtroom, we all stood as Judge Lambert entered. She motioned for us to sit and instructed Kent to stand. His attorney stood beside him.

"This is a grievous crime. The court doesn't have the resources to undo the harm that was caused. As Ms. Frank so eloquently stated, a life has been lost. That cannot be changed. I would add that Genevieve Sanders' life was brutally and callously taken in a manner that caused suffering. The impact on the families and on this community is profound. Do you wish to address the court before you are sentenced?" The judge asked Larsen.

Whispered conversations could be heard throughout the courtroom. His lawyer spoke up. "I have advised my client against speaking to the court. However, he is choosing to go against my advice."

The judge simply nodded to Kent.

He turned away from the judge and toward the audience. "There are no heroes here, and there never were. If the system were just, everyone would be alive. The man who should be sitting in this chair is right there." He pointed his finger at me.

The audience murmured shocked and outraged responses until the judge called for order. "Do you have any comments about the length of your sentence?" she prodded.

"My sentence has already been served."

This brought another round of murmurs.

"Mr. Larsen, I accept your plea of guilty to both counts of the indictment and sentence you to the upper range of forty-eight years and sixty-eight years on each count to be served consecutively. I further order that half of your prison wages shall be used to support victims of violent crime. You are hereby committed to the Commissioner of Corrections. I also want to make it very clear to you that if Minnesota didn't have strong sentencing guidelines, I would be sentencing you to two consecutive life sentences without the possibility of parole. The public isn't going to understand the subtleties of sentencing, and that is in essence what you are facing here. Please take him away."

The audience exploded into conversation as the defendant was escorted out of the courtroom. Judge Lambert watched the reactions for a short minute before taking leave to her chambers.

Georgia turned to me. "In light of Kent's comments, I agree completely with the sentencing."

I nodded.

"That guy tested positive for a crazy mix of drugs, but that doesn't excuse him for what he did. He had free rein in the evidence room. We'll probably never know exactly what he used to achieve his goals."

Georgia knew from her brief visit to the emergency room that her system showed traces of a mix of downers and synthetics. Andrea was still hospitalized, but the doctors were making slow progress in clearing her system of the drugs. Kennedy joined us in the hallway, and we all agreed to drop by the hospital for a visit on our way home.

Something I Had To Say

Chapter 29

I knew I had something to make right with Smitty. Yes, the guy could be a jerk in a lot of ways, but he had done his best to help me find Georgia. All through the case, I certainly had serious doubts about him and had even wondered if he was the serial killer. Georgia and I decided it would be best for us to invite him over to the house for a barbecue. We also invited Kennedy, who accepted the invitation and asked if she could bring a guest. She kept us in suspense until she showed up with Michael King, the lie guy who had helped assess Gant's interrogation.

I manned the grill with Smitty and Michael over beers, while Georgia and Kennedy worked and laughed in the kitchen with wine.

I hadn't really planned on being friends with Smitty, but

we had been through a lot, and I felt guilty for assuming the worst about him. I owed him this dinner and planned on being honest with him if the topic came up. I thought it ironic that we were trying to rebuild things in the company of the local expert on lies.

Once Michael, Smitty, and I were settled on the back patio, I realized that it was my responsibility to be direct about how I had misjudged Smitty. I asked Michael if he could give us a minute.

"Sure, I think I'm needed in the kitchen, "he said.

"Smitty, I owe you an apology." I watched him for a reaction. Also to see if he knew this was coming.

"I'm listening," he said.

"I'm sorry I doubted you."

"Doubted me how?" He wasn't letting me off easy.

"I let my doubts cloud how I saw you during the investigation."

"What made you doubt me?" he persisted, sounding a little agitated.

"I let your attitude about women creep into how capable I saw you during the investigation."

"I knew that, "he said.

"I was off base. I apologize," I said, without going into detail. He didn't need to know the full extent of my suspicion that he was a sick and twisted serial killer.

"That's why you assigned Corey to me?"

"Pretty much. But I also think you were trying to do too much alone."

"So, how bad did you think I was?"

"I didn't know." I wasn't going to let this apology turn into something really negative. That wasn't my intent. "I think we know each other better now."

"No sweat, man. I know I'm messed up. I mean, two tours

of combat and losing my wife. Who wouldn't be screwed up, right? Sometimes I've made an ass out of myself acting like a dog. I get it, you know?"

I nodded—shocked that he actually saw that in himself.

He looked at me eye to eye for perhaps the first time since we had been partnered up.

"You have your good points, too," I said with a smile, and asked him to let the rest of the group know that the steaks were done. We weren't going to be best friends, but we might make it as partners.

Moving On

Chapter 30

Georgia and I hadn't decided whether to move or stay put, but we would see how the next few months played out for us. We both still found it hard to get to green light vulnerability in a place that had been violated by a serial killer. By the same token, we both wanted to try to reclaim the space. We needed to make it ours again. Maybe a few more house parties would help bring some normalcy back into our lives.

Meanwhile, throughout the summer, we spent more time outdoors wandering the many city trails that bordered the creeks and riverbeds of the city. Our house was gradually beginning to feel like home again, but the Rose Garden would never be the same for us. I would never be able to avoid the intrusional memories. Where most find solace and peace, I would forever remember the horrors and gruesome past that was now my reality.

On one of our walks, we took a break on a boulder overlooking Congdon Creek. It was a warm night with a slight breeze, and we could see a tiny slice of Lake Superior off in the distance. I got down on one knee, reached into my pocket, and produced an engagement ring. With hands shaking, I asked her if she would do me the honor and privilege of marrying me. She accepted.

We were in no rush to get home, as I had been on paid administrative leave since Larsen was locked up. We walked slowly down the dim trail, taking our time and enjoying the moment. She talked about what kind of wedding she wanted, and I listened, just happy to hear her happy.

As we continued to walk, I began to reflect on the case. It had been three months since Larsen was sentenced. Paid leave can't last forever. That was a long time for someone to be off work and getting paid, and I knew that must have been tearing up the powers that be. Of chief concern to the department was my going rogue after being taken off the case. The news coverage had been favorable toward me, Georgia, and the department for stopping the killing spree, and now having the killer safely behind bars. I wasn't sure I still wanted to be a cop. The DPD was either going to promote me, fire me, or counsel me out. I knew firing me was out of the question because of the widespread news coverage. Channel 7 had even interviewed Alex, and public opinion held that we were some kind of a hero family.

The final disposition happened three weeks after the trial at the City Council meeting. The room was packed, and a hungry media mob waited outside the building. Local stations and CNN were filming the whole proceeding. The room buzzed with excitement and tension as the Council chair opened the meeting and suspended the remainder of the agenda until my matter was resolved. My union attorney was seated to my right. He informed me that there would be no hearing. They were offering me my job back.

The captain looked stressed. I got the feeling he wasn't happy about it. I watched the dog and pony show, said nice things about the department to the media, and arranged to meet with the captain on Monday morning. I spent the weekend alternating between working out and preparing for the meeting, with Georgia's help.

I wasn't ready to go back to the violent crimes unit. Georgia helped me to realize that I wanted a duty change to head up the traffic unit. I put together a proposal and prepared myself to meet with the captain.

He didn't stand or shake my hand when I entered his office. Both he and the chief sat at a large table, and I took a seat across from them.

"Gentlemen," I greeted them. The captain looked like he wanted to fire me on the spot, but the politics might not be giving him that option.

"We'd like to offer you a promotion to sergeant," he said, much to my surprise. My captain's face was red.

"I'd rather go fishing," I said, unable to articulate my carefully prepared proposal.

"Excuse me?" His face turned a brighter red.

I took some pleasure in toying with him. "Traffic. It's my favorite kind of police work. I call it fishing." He calmed down a bit.

"How the hell can I promote you to traffic?"

"I could identify high accident areas, and cover those areas that the statistics reveal to be especially dangerous. I could coordinate with other departments and the State Patrol to monitor the high traffic holiday and peak season travel. I think there are federal grants that would look favorably on interdepartmental coordination and DWI enforcement and prevention. Maybe we could put together media blitzes to increase seatbelt use. I could capitalize on my media recognition."

"Not going to happen," the captain said flatly.

My stress level amped up. *Was I going to be put in a desk job, where I could be kept out of any potential rogue cop situations, but where I would wither and die of boredom?*

"I'm assigning you to homicide. You brought down a serial killer, and now you have the experience we need in that unit."

I sat in stunned silence. *How many more horrific events can my psyche handle? How will this affect my marriage to Georgia? How the hell can I do what I did for Georgia over and over again? It's not the same when it's not personal. This isn't where I wanted this to go.*

"What do you say?" he asked.

"Not sure," I replied honestly. "I'll see how it goes."

"Good. I put some cold cases in your in-box. See what rocks you can turn over until the next big homicide comes in."

Cold cases. That I could do, for now.

A *Tip of the Hat*, from Marcus Bruning

Jen taught to me to look at people in a kind and caring way and to never give up. When dealing with those who had committed crime, Jen fought to be the endless voice of the victim and to keep the focus of the criminal justice system squarely on the criminal. Never looking to the victim's behavior or actions as cause or in any way responsible. Jen has always been passionate in her work, especially with young people and victims of domestic and sexual violence, ensuring they are validated and guided toward good, kindness and the compassion they needed and deserve.

In writing this book, I brought much of the story, pulling from the many experiences I had throughout my career. In some ways it was difficult to write due to the troubling visuals in my mind where people were hurting so deeply. In other ways it was refreshing to bring the reader into the mindset of those who serve. Jen brought the detail of the surrounding and the story's connection to the reader. We exchanged the book weekly and couldn't wait to read what the other had contributed.

I will always admire and cherish Jen, her infectious smile and love for life. I learned something fascinating each time I was with her and will never forget the time she gave me. When I learned the treatment options for Jen's illness had been exhausted one morning in November 2015, my heart ached. Jen told me her life expectancy and I wept at the finality of losing my friend. How could a heart this big ever be silenced by an indiscriminate disease called cancer?

Find peace my friend, Marcus

Marcus Bruning

Bruning retired in 2013 to a home on the Mississippi River near Bemidji, Minnesota after 28 years in Law Enforcement. Marcus served the last 20 years with the St. Louis County Sheriff's Office in Duluth, Minnesota where he retired as Supervising Deputy Sheriff (Rank of Major).

Marcus Bruning is known for the real world practical education and training he provides for law enforcement professionals across the country. Bruning is nationally recognized as an expert on law enforcement response to intimate partner abuse, sexual assault and stalking and has presented training in all fifty states.

Major Bruning has published articles in the National Sheriff's Magazine and has been quoted in Oprah's "O" Magazine.

Jen Wright

Wright is the author of the popular Jo Spence mystery novels. She lives in Clover Valley, a small community located northeast of Duluth near the north shore of Lake Superior. She shares life with her partner, Kari, and their loving canine companions in a community of friends.

Wright is Superintendent of the Arrowhead Juvenile Center, Arrowhead Regional Corrections where she has worked for ARC for 29 years. She has trained in the areas of Domestic Violence, Gender responsive services, Drug Courts, and Juvenile Probation issues

Jen has a BA degree in Sociology with a concentration in Criminology and course work towards a Masters in Public Administration.

For more information on this title, and for other books from Riverfeet Press, you can find us online.

www.riverfeetpress.com

https://www.facebook.com/riverfeetbooks

RIVERFEET
PRESS